HOLY SMOKE

HOLY SMOKE

by

Fanny Howe

Drawings by Colleen McCallion

FICTION COLLECTIVE, INC.   NEW YORK

First edition
Copyright ©1979 by Fanny Howe
All rights reserved

Library of Congress Catalog No. 78-68130
ISBN: 0-914590-54-5 (hardcover)
ISBN: 0-914590-55-3 (paperback)

Published by FICTION COLLECTIVE, INC.
Production by Coda Press, Inc.
Distributed by George Braziller, Inc.
One Park Avenue
New York, N.Y. 10016

Acknowledgment is made to Bob Perelman's *Hills* for publishing a portion of *Holy Smoke.*

All characters in this book are fictional.

This publication is in part made possible with support from the National Endowment of the Arts in Washington, D.C., a Federal agency, the New York State Council on the Arts, Brooklyn College, and the Teachers and Writers Collabrative.

1. Dialectic of Site and Nonsite

Site	*Nonsite*
1. Open limits	Closed Limits
2. A series of Points	An Array of Matter
3. Outer Coordinates	Inner Coordinates
4. Subtraction	Addition
5. Indeterminate Certainty	Determinate Uncertainty
6. Scattered Information	Contained Information
7. Reflection	Mirror
8. Edge	Center
9. Some Place (physical)	No Place (abstract)
10. Many	One

Range of Convergence

from THE SPIRAL JETTY by
Robert Smithson

Last night I dreamed I had a name. It was Anon.
My parents gave it to me. They sat in the back of my cab.
I saw them, alive again! through the rearview mirror,
soft and smiling. Where I was taking them, I do not know.
Where they came from, a mystery. Why they said,
"Your real name is Anon," I'll never know.

We drove through a landscape I'm sure I've seen before:
On the right (East) a deep river, black and thick.
On the left (West) green sloping fields.
My longing to turn to speak to them was haltered by a terrible
anxiety: we might drive into that river, should I turn my head.

In this rigid frame of mind, I drove on to daybreak. The
crash of garbage pails.

J was found dead today. He is always being found dead, of
course, but I never dared write it down before.
But now that I have a name, I know I must write.
"Song is existence. Easy for the gods," wrote Rilke.
I'm scared, but feel it is time to be really bad.

The Blue Boys came, as always, with J's mug shot, and
asked,
"Is this your man?"
Yes, I said, since it always is.
Later Jimmy himself told me he would turn me in, if I wrote
anything down,—or leave.
So I wrote it down and feel like Euridice returning with
a sword. The Muse who slew the Singer!

My little statue of the Virgin Mary said: "What is mightier
than the sword? The pen is, the penis, or the pun is. Take
your pick, lady."

She's a character.

I'm a virgin again at last.
There may not be a new hymen, there may still be a scar
where my skin tore in labor, but fifteen years of celibacy
must add up to some kind of freedom.
James approves of my condition, but condemns the attitude
behind it.
    "You must want everyone to say how good you
    are," he says, "because you've turned your back on
    the people, on revolution. You need a sweet image
    to compensate."
But I don't care if people think I'm good. Only strong!
    "Ha. Everyone cares. Only a few people dare be
    overtly nasty. The heroes."
What am I doing wrong?
    "The books you read—poetry, esoteric shit, philo-
    sophy. You've dropped out."
What difference does it make what I read?
    "On your death bed, will you be able to say, I
    helped the poor in their struggle for justice?

Or will you only be able to quote Baudelaire?"
Either case would be pompous.
   "You understand, I'm here to quarrel, not to
   praise."
Yes, yes, I understand.

I pulled in fifty bucks today. Mostly messenger service,
which means I get some exercise on the elevators. I'm
building up a regular clientele. Once I've got that, I
won't need to hustle, no more. Black veins at daybreak
on the windowpanes, skin of my home, one tree's black
webbing.

Once I've got what I want, will I want what I have? This
pursuit of money is a tribulation. Now I can say I am
doing it for my daughter, but when she leaves,
which will be soon, what can I say? What will I have to
live for? The pursuit of truth and wisdom is a full-time
occupation, but I'll have to make money too. I'll have to
drive the car around Manhattan, I'll have to talk to strangers, I'll have to listen.

The other night I took an elderly railroad worker home,
and he was quoting e.e. cummings all the way uptown.
"The country hasn't come to terms with cummings yet,"
he told me with great spirit, "too much attention on Whitman."
So we had to continue this conversation over whiskey,
in an Irish bar, for we were both stunned by our lack
of solitude.
Today was a glorious day—the January thaw—blue sky—
sunshine & warm. Every season but fall is a pain in this city.
It was a day just like this when James the First was wasted.
And the day before, when we were planning the hold-up and
he kept saying, *If the apple's ripe, Time falls.* It was fall.
And the day after, when I was in the slams, didn't have the

kid any more, they had taken her screaming off to
Separation City. And when she left her name was Pepita,
and when she returned her name was Pepsi. Six years old,
and nearly a stranger, having all the mannerisms of a family
I never knew. How all our parents are strangers Time
selects for us, and how children survive the most dreadful
people!

Still I say it's a glorious feeling, though the prison sensation
never leaves me. You pass through all the locked doors
coming out and lock the car door, going away, and space has
locks & keys, apartments, friendships, minds and words.
Home is just your chosen prison and the only freedom left
comes from feeling you are on the track of Truth.

THE MATERIAL WORLD

Just as antlers appear to bear no relation to the soft body of
the deer, so the snowy petals of dogwood appear to bear no
relation to the leaves & branches from which they spring.
Red cardinals flash through the trees, again composed of
strange material certainly not wooden. Dogwood snowing
on the china blue sky. Green leaves brilliant and transparent
in the spring. My green might be your blue, but the patterns
would be satisfying, and the same. Certain monkeys have
speckled reddish hair that approaches feathering. Out of
the dirt, comes grass. "The flag of my disposition," Whitman
calls it. And he is not one for metaphors. If you separated
each well-formed particle of life from its origin, you would
have as good as you've got. Feathers growing on trees. Fish
with beaks. Fountains spurting from the temples of elks.
Dogwood petals fluttering from the cheeks of monkeys.
And once you had analysed the property of each particle, it
would all make perfect sense!

January 14th. Freezing cold, a film of ice on the rooftops
& trees. At six a.m. a gentleman called to say that Jimmy had
been found dead—This time in the hopper of a Penn
Central train, travelling between New York and New
Haven. I was asked to identify him at the morgue, but said I
couldn't handle it.

"Can you give me some unusual feature," asked the
man, "for positive identification?"

Then I went out so I wouldn't know either way. But then I
came back in, wanting to know. It was him. The gentleman
said that J was travelling on the 6:10 train from Penn
Station, was found about an hour later by a ticket collector
who saw him go into the hopper right after
the train took off, thought he was a deadhead
trying to bum a free ride. He was shot in the head this time.
They took his body off at Bridgeport.

"Dispose of him as you would any old indigent,"
I said.

I know he was on his way to Boston, with all the others, to
participate in the busing rally there. Tomorrow is Martin
Luther King Day.

January 15. Bitterly cold but bright. Pepsi had no school, so
she came down to Penn Station with me. In the meantime,
Josephine packed up J's clothes, so I wouldn't have to see or
touch them, but his papers she was not allowed to touch.
Pepsi and I decided to pretend we were J's wife and child,
then ride the train to New Haven, talking to people.
Early morning, the station crawling with bag ladies
and doped-up individuals in rotten clothes. I found
a slick conductor who knew all about it. He drew us
over to a quiet area near the phone booths to avoid
a scene. Pepsi looked like a real orphan in her blue jeans and
leather, black curls falling down from under her cap,
mooning.
    "Look," said the conductor softly, "Your best bet is
to hop the next train to Boston. You'll find a young
man in the club car, comes from France or something. The sleazy type. He knows what happened."
So we got on the 8:10. Settled in the club car, and ordered
tea & Danish. The guy was there all right, just like the other
jack described him. He must have been around twenty,
slender, oozing & sensual, he took a fancy to Pepsi, and sat
with us, when I told him who we were.
    "Oohh, I'm very sorry what happened," he said.
What *did* happen, I asked. His eyes were two muddy pools of
obsequiem, if there's such a word, as he told his tale.
    "I saw him slip into the water closet," is how his tale
began, "and I kept an eye on the door, it's what

we are supposed to do, you understand, and then I saw
another person slip in after him, a beautiful woman,
and this was pretty *bizarre*, because, you understand, it is a water closet for one, heh, heh, and then
she came out, but he did not, so I mentioned this to
Ronald the brakeman, who went into the john
and found your husband there, and he had
his round trip ticket in his hand—"
Okay, okay, I said, but what about the woman? Did you tell
the cops about her?
   "But of course!" he cried, hands up. "And I can
tell you, in strict detail, how she resembled. She
was dressed in a soft, maybe cashmere, cream-
colored coat with a rabbit-fur collar. High heels.
Slim ankles. Blond frosted hair. Red lipstick and
nails. She was just carrying a purse, no baggage, an
alligator purse, so she was, you understand, a
wealthy kind of woman. On the other hand, her
face, you see, was very dark, possibly belonging to a
woman of African origin, though I only got a quick
look, it was all so fast. She did not look like the kind
to shoot anyone, no, but you can never tell, can you."
Never, I agreed, but wished I could lay eyes on this extra-
ordinary woman. Maybe a spurned mistress, maybe a spy,
but a woman all the same. I was going to smile when I saw
his ankle rubbing up against Pepsi's, under the table. I gave
him a sharp kick, and we got off the train at Rye.

Back home, I found, in Jimmy's papers, a quote (his or
whose?) reading: "Our lowest, or least perfect, actions are
attempts at originality. Our best are conscious imitations of
those we admire."

IS DEATH EVIL?

If there is a Life before life, probably Death is not evil, but simply a temporary condition. If, however, life begins at conception, Death is evil, because it obliterates the little we have learned. Not fair! One does not wish to make contact with Death, by murder or by illness, we all know this, and only those who believe there is a Life before life can handle the dread of Death. In other words, most of us feel, instinctively, that Death is evil, that it, literally, describes Evil. And so we will do anything to avoid it. We will not kill men or flies. Yet villains abound! The carriers of Death. Twisted & diabolical people. Out of pain, they inflict more pain. And who can shower them with pity, forgiveness, love? They should be ashamed of themselves. But only their victims have the right to forgive them; no one else. And it is the victim, alone, who understands that there is a Life before life—even if that Life is called History—and that victim is the only one who understands that Death is a temporary condition, as pain is, as Evil is, as Christ was simply a condition arising from Mary's virginity. The victim is the most powerful individual on earth, when he or she decides to use that power to conquer the villains. The carriers of Death. I am that victim.

(Who wrote this?)

Pepsi is upset for many reasons. First, she is later than any of her friends, getting her period. But it's now about to come. And second, the endless comings and goings of J are aggravating. She grieves and recovers, grieves and recovers, and blames a lot of it on me. "You don't know how to handle him," she tells me. Or, "I wish they'd use a more effective weapon on his head. Why don't you tell them that?"

But it's out of my control, and I have no relationship with Thems of any sort any more. Byron said, "In solitude we are least alone," but Burke said, "An entire life of solitude contradicts the purpose of our being, since death itself is scarcely an idea of more terror." Mr. Simms said, "The true life of man is in society." Von Zimmerman elaborated, saying, "Those beings only are fit for solitude, who like nobody and are liked by nobody." But the Virgin Mary countered these gentlemen with her usual grace, saying "Blessed are the lonely, for they shall speak to statues."

"You are entirely gonzo nutso bananas," Pepsi said, "and I think I'll run away."
In an hour she got in bed with me and asked me to read aloud the Marguerite poems of Matthew Arnold.

Perplexing, unresolved weather today. In a little notebook, Jimmy had written:
Richard Nixon has been a Communist since the
late Forties. Am I the only one who knows?
A pale, snowy day, Monday, drear and damp. Wet streets, had to be careful gliding through the park. Quit with $32 in my bag and a filthy hangover. Went home, took Alka-Seltzer and got in bed with Rilke. On the inside of the jacket, J had scrawled: "People think they have to obey all their instincts! But you don't *have* to, just because you want to! Wow!" And then the phone rang. It was a man called Lucas, sounded like a life insurance salesman, full of beans, a

musical fruit, said he wanted to come see me about the Jimmy business. I got out of bed, swilled a beer and waited.

Lucas shuffled in around two and made himself right at home in the livingroom, like one of my elderly neighbors coming in to talk about the pipes. Small and stuffy with dilated nostrils, delicate fingers. He opened a briefcase and took out a walkie-talkie, among other objects.

"This is to keep in touch with my buddie outside," he explained politely.

Then he produced some snapshots—two mug shots, some family scenes, one beside a car, one in a California setting.

"Are you this woman?" he asked.

Some of them I am, some of them I'm not, I said.

"Don't get hysterical, Dear, please. We're not out to hurt you, whoever you are. But you were a friend of James List, alias Jimbo Lightfoot, J.B. Ford, Jaime Lopez—?"

His eyes twinkled merrily. My ears felt like hands on the accordian of my brain, squeezing and pulling out strange, loud melodies.

"Did you know he was a fugitive?" he asked.

No.

"Grand larceny. Arizona."

What's that got to do with me?

"Don't look so scared."

Wouldn't you?

"I wouldn't ask for trouble like you do. I wouldn't
consort with hippies, drug addicts and radicals. I
wouldn't marry a third-rate bank robber. I wouldn't
end up in the clinker. Not if I was a mother first.
And you're a mother first, aren't you, Dear?"

Sure thing, I said.

"James List was not just a big-time burglar. He was
a paid informer. He was working for us in exchange
for a clean record. We think the Cubans might have
killed him."

Why don't you ask the French waiter?

"That was no French waiter, Dear. That was a
Cuban. He's gone. Took a train south after you
spoke to him, we can't trace him."

So, get to the point.

"You want to get back in the mainstream, right?"

Right.

"It's like talking to a man talking to you, Dear, I
like that."

I bet.

"We could use your help."

I've got a big mouth. I'll tell my friends.

"You don't know who your friends are, Dear, that's
the whole point," and he chortled.

My ears began to thrum strange melodies again. Fear is un-
fitting to a woman in my circumstances, so I got up and
asked him, please, to leave.

"I'll leave, but it would save you *mucho* time, if you
would cooperate. I mean, truthfully, Dear, it's not
going to be a case of wine and roses, if you don't give us
your help. We need your friend Jim's property. His
papers, notebooks, clothes. We need it now, in order to
track down various individuals. Please be a lamb and say
yes."

No.
"But why not?"
He left it to me. It's all mine.
"Bullshit."
Out!
I pointed an imperious finger down the hall and he packed
away his papers and rose to his feet.
"You'll be sorry," he said, like a little boy.
No way.
"You said you were a mother first. Well, that's not
going to be the case for long."
Out!
He left. I've been sitting around since, eating Oreos,
thinking: He will pluck the meat from the shell. He will
scrape the honey from the pot. He will drain the water
from the pool. He will pull the placenta from the wall.
He will eat the egg inside out.

A wet Saturday, drenching rain, grey & warm, seems like spring, causes people to do weird things, like buy lipstick or go insane. So in order to forget about the man's threats, I went shopping for underclothes. Bought silk panties for the kid, then stopped at a deli for lunch. A middle-aged couple, obviously mental patients, eating at the next table. The stooped bodies of prisoners, misshapen skulls, as if from trying to squeeze their way out through the bars, both over-weight. Sloppy with the food. The man wild-eyed despair, the woman moronic and pale. But they spoke ordinary English to each other, mayonnaise all over their chins. They knew how to do things, but didn't seem to like doing them. "The indifferent universe." When no one loves you, the world is a blank stare. Those two must have met in the hospital. Both wore rings. Maybe marriage had brought them to this state—marriage to others or to each other, it doesn't matter. The irreparable damage caused by forced acquaintance. When the other does *not* become invisible, does *not* become habitual. Instead, a busted shoe, a blister. I began to get that overshaded feeling, watching them. Then my car gave out on 43rd and Broadway. Felt the trouble coming for days. No breakdown lane on Broadway. Left a note on the windshield and ran to the garage. When I came back, a rookie cop was leaning on the hood. He waited, with me, for the tow truck, then asked me to have a drink. You can never be dowdy enough. Or fashions in people change too.

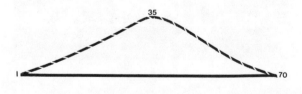

A Healthy Life Span

No one did nothing. Or someone did something. Nobody
said nothing to nobody. Or everyone said something to
someone else. That is, my child is gone. Gone! Someone
took her away. Her school friends saw her go—
Off in a blue florist truck, full of flowers as if for a
funeral.
Grotesque arrangements of lily, orchid, iris, macaroon tints.
The funeral smell of marzipan. Almond.
All mine, gone.

I thought I may be wrong and ran home. Searched every
room under beds and in closets, but there was no one there.
I asked myself, maybe she was always gone?
I was alone and imagined an offspring?
I dragged a ghost around with me and everyone smiled
behind their hands?
No one is nowhere. No one did nothing. Nobody did
nothing to no one. No one said nothing.

"Analyze those phrases again," said J, "and you've
got something. Someone who could be anywhere."
He was clipping his nails, seated on the closed toilet seat.
"I told you," he continued, "When the Muse grabs
the pen away from the artist and begins to draw
designs herself, she can only draw herself. This is
dangerous. She draws herself and turns into her
drawing. Her image becomes herself, her life com-
pletes the shadows and substance. Her instincts
are always correct, and out of control."
I took the shower hose and turned it full on his head, and
burned him out, till he was no more than a butt in a tray or
a flush in the can. Then I girded up my loins for the call
of the wilderness.

(Maybe he's right?)

The only lead I had was Lucas.
But first I wandered the streets—East, West, South, North—
and called all Pepsi's friends.
This assured me that I did, in fact, have a daughter, for they
all knew who I was talking about.
　　"She got in the truck voluntarily."
　　"She looked like she knew the guy."
　　"He was dark-skinned, but that's all I saw."
　　"Gloves, he wore gloves."
　　"They headed towards Roosevelt Drive. East."
　　"I saw them curve back, West."
　　"She waved goodbye. You know. Cheerfully."

I waited twenty-four hours. And more.
　　　　　　　　Parent Hood
　　　　　　　　Child Hood
　　　　　　　　Robin Hood
　　　　　　　　Hood's Milk
　　　　　　　　A Hood
　　　　　　　　Mother Hood
　　　　　　　　Cape & Hood
　　　　　　　　Red Riding Hood
　　　　　　　　Mount Hood
　　　　　　　　Hooded Eyes
HOOD: A soft, flexible covering for head and neck.
　　A cover for the entire head of a hawk, used when
　　the bird is not in pursuit of game.
　　A native English suffix denoting state, condition,
　　character.

HOODWINKED

Mother Hood and her daughter, Child Hood, lived in. That is, in exchange for room and board, they cleaned, cooked and babysat for the Rich family. Super Rich and Nouveau Rich were the parents of Inherited-Wealth Rich and Got Rich.

One day Child Hood ran away, or was bustled away by accident. Mother Hood let a week pass by before she dared tell Mr. Rich what had happened. It was a form of paralysis taking place inside her hood, where no one could see. She was afraid she had made a mistake, and she hoped she had made a mistake. So time passed and Child Hood was absorbed into the outside world. Hidden from Mother Hood!

When Super Rich heard the news, he called the police. He felt sorry for poor Mother Hood and wanted his house in order again. Besides, he desired the gratitude of someone poor, in case there was such a thing as Heaven and that he wanted too.

But the police were at a loss. The world is so big and full of people! Round, round. They didn't know where to begin looking and got bored. After all!

In the end it was up to Mother Hood to cover the globe. For no one else really cared. This was the horrible fact of the matter. No one but she really needed Child Hood! In the whole world, this is the saddest truth, accounting for the suffix Hood, which shields the truth from even the bright lights of the stars.

For there is no greater loss than the loss of a child—to the world's hoodwinkery. To the arms of the galaxies. To being shadowed by the hood of Nothingness.

A thaw, and loss of paralysis. I have covered this entire city, daily, driving and craning my head to see the image of Pepsi, on the streets. She's nowhere. Around. Here. So I took the card that Lucas gave me and headed over to Broadway and 54th Street. My car was packed with clothes, books, food, drink and ammunition. The point is, not to give in. To find her without giving in. To do it alone. I know Them: If I give in, They will take her farther away and ask for more. And then I will have to give more and more. No more! Now is the moment to say No.

It was the kind of building where they keep men like Lucas. It could have been anywhere in the United States. Not tall & sleek with elevators, not dingy & foul. Halfway between. Dentist, a ballet school, Knights of Columbus, a podiatrist. A wooden odor. Wide staircase with a worn but shining bannister. He was located on the third floor, his name was on the door, no indication of occupation or rank. A blue-haired secretary in a purple dress reading REDBOOK.

"What do you want," she said irritably.

Mr. Lucas.

"Just knock and go in."

So I knocked and he called me in. He looked like he had just finished jerking off under his desk. His expression, when he saw me, expressed nostalgia and some guilt.

"You changed your mind?"

No, I'm just looking around.

"For what?"

My kid.

"As I told you, Dear, you're already in *mucho* trouble. You don't want to end up behind bars, I know that, so you only have to say the word and I'll call the boss."

Who's the boss? I'll call him.

He rubbed his neck where there might have hung a noose just a few minutes ago, he looked rotten. I sat on the edge of his desk, my legs were weak, but his were weaker, he didn't stand up once.

"Look," he begged, "just sit tight at your apartment and we'll get in touch with you. Your daughter won't be hurt, but the sooner you give us that property, the better. For you and her."

Just one hint where she is? I whined.

He wriggled around in his chair and began to shuffle papers. I followed his hands, looking for clues in the litter. He was shaking his head like a very old dog with a flea in his ear, but I knew he was backed up by others more vicious, and I must not weaken.

"I'm sorry, Dear, I really feel for you."

Just one hint?

"I can't help you."

Are you Catholic?

"What do you mean?"

I mean, do you believe in an Afterlife?

He gave me a haunted, disappointed look, and I glanced down and picked up a piece of paper which had a letter-head—CASTRO CARS—popular among the litter on his desk. He snatched it away, but not before my brain devoured the address, Boston.

"You can leave now," he said.

But you haven't answered my question.

"Scram."

I left obediently, but it was the last command I'll follow. I keep saying to myself, Resist, Resist. They'll invent one more test for me, no matter what I do. This is why I only ask of myself that I be a complete bitch. Mean is holy!

January 15, Boston.

The clouds scudding incredibly fast and low overhead, the buildings, if you look up, are like ships sailing over the sea. Coolish, really. I went to Mass at a Franciscan chapel which contained a very pretty statue of the Virgin Mary. I'm sure, this time, I heard her speak.

"Blessed is the Fruit of the Loom, all women of the garment district. The lilies of the field don't know how to sew."

I am staying with R in a suburb of Boston. He's getting me a wig, a new license for the car and registration. Tomorrow I'll hit CASTRO CARS.

This letter turned up in J's things:

People,

I have been angry since birth at the way you have treated me. It is one thing not to be able to forgive someone for his past and his future in advance; it is another to consciously abuse the opportunity of a person to transform himself, to grow. Not fair! You never loved me, you never forgave me, you saw my history and you ridiculed me, you made fun of me, and now you reject me with sympathy. Pain!

Yes, the first slave-trader was not as evil as you, for you don't even need to keep me this way. There is no excuse. Or maybe you have an excuse: you have to keep people poor and dependent in order to enjoy your power. If you had no poor, you would not know who you were! Much of it is psychological, yes it is. I do not see it as all economic any more.

For I loved you! I was at the mercy of your power, your grace, your beauty. I craved your attention and affection, but it never came. You never approved of me, whatever I did. If I copied you, I was a fool. If I fought you, I was 'a criminal element.' So what then, what now?

I am an artist. And you are Kafka's father. You are Cinderella's stepsisters—"cold, unmoved and to temptation slow." Now I am the fly in your ointment. The right thing for the wrong reason and the wrong thing for the right reason. I am the X in your alphabet. I am the calories in your blueberry muffin. I am the toxic fumes in your energetic factories. I am the mosquito outside your resort house. I do not need to act, to lift a finger, I only need to stay. sauntering among your belongings, like a thief who never steals, I do not need to work, I only need to stay awake on the sidelines. Yes, constant vigilance! I am the bad beginning that brings the bad end.

And then I found THE CODE:

Anemone	Pinky Purple	F	450
Butterfly Weed	Orange	M	225
Chicory	Blue	A	75
Dandelion	Yellow	J	1500
Evening Primrose	Pale Yellow	J	4500
Fireweed	Purplish Pink	F	150
Goldenrod	Yellow	J	2300
Harebell	Bright Blue	A	520
Oxalis	White & Red	M	70
Phlox	Lilac	O	450
Xyris	Yellow	J	2000
Queen Anne's Lace	White	F	225

And at the bottom of the page: THE FIDUCIARY

A fine clear Monday.
It sounded like a birthday party at dawn: toots, honks, twirts, beeps—just birds waking up.
R presented me with a blond wig and the right papers; then

we kissed goodbye.
I was prickling with fear, until, on my way to Castro
Cars, I remembered the Virgin, whose gaze is the gaze of
Consciousness—
A gaze that absorbs even the scared consciousness of the
infant on her lap and floats beyond him.
After all, she came first!
And what a comfort She is in times of trouble, as the Beatles
so truly sang, leveling the cruel with her permanent eyes.

CASTRO CARS—Rows of glitter, outside and in. A body
shop behind. In front, streams of traffic and slush. I roamed
around, looking like the Lady on the Train in my wig and
pretty clothes. Smiled warmly at all the salesmen, and pretended to be interested in a little second-hand Ghia. I
sensed, the whole time, that I would not have to seek anyone
out, but would be approached myself, as one always is in
such places, but this time by the Boss. I could be sure I was
being followed at all times. It took awhile, and then a guy in
a shiny suit and face came over and asked me to step
into the office.
    "Are you looking for a car or a person?" he asked.
I've got a car.
    "That's what I thought."
Then why did you ask?
    "I'm just warning you."
Please—just one hint.
He laughed a little.
Am I getting warmer? I asked, to make him laugh some more.
    "Colder, colder."
Then I should head south?
    "You're nuts, lady, nuts," he laughed.
Do you believe in the Immaculate Coneption?

"What?"

I'm serious—

"Listen, sister, you're not going to find nothing
   here. We just deal in cars."

He moved from desk to door. But I wanted him to know I
was a mean mother, so I pulled my gun on him.

Just one hint, I insisted.

Men don't like to see a woman with a gun in her hand. He
backed off, scared.

Just one hint, I said.

"I dunno, I swear I dunno—"

Sure you do.

"Something to do with a Sergeant Pepper."

Where's he?

"I dunno, they'll kill me."

Sergeant Pepper, I said.

"Please don't hurt me."

He backed against his desk and slid around the side of it
towards his chair. I thought he was going to have a heart
attack and twirled my pistol once, before snapping it back
in my bag. He started forward.

Down, Rover, I said.

He sat down.

That's the boy. I headed for my car and shot out of the
place, fast. Weak, weak, I had been too weak!

Scrambled for awhile over a bony beach, knuckles of rock
under my bare feet, felt good. Sometimes physical pain is
the only kind to be had. Then I went to an old bar-and-
grille in Lynn, where Pedro, my old friend the code-inter-
preter works. He's a yellowish fellow with many moles &
gold teeth, squinting humorous eyes & slightly buck teeth.
He was cleaning the counter top when I came in. Fixed me
a good tall double-shot of scotch. When I showed him J's
code, he said
  "Can't do it anymore, my friend."
Ah shit.
  "But I know someone who can," he said, "A hippie
  freak, part of some religious order, north of
  here, New Hampshire, he can do it."
He scrawled down the name of a Hart Christian on a slip of
paper, and the address.
  "They'll give you bed and board and try to convert
  you to Christianity. Know what I mean?"
I could guess.
Drove north through a beautiful snowscape, desolation,
glacial mounds. Strange feelings again, that maybe I had
made a mistake, misinterpreted all events of the recent past,
and there was no reason for me to be where I was.
A psychotic break?
Housewives' disease, or Agoraphobia, swelled through me.
As if the ribbons had been snapped before the Christening
ceremony and the boat was adrift, and nameless.
What is this thing called life?
What are those trees doing there?
The snow was the queerest of phenomena, and Being a
small sac over Nothinghood.

Cold and clear, Tuesday. The so-called Christian Converts
are chopping down trees for firewood. They have been up
since 5 a.m. Cold showers, prayers. I ate oatmeal with them

at six. They wear huge heavy crosses, men and women, and worship the Virgin Mary. A statue of Herself shadows the snow in front of this white farmhouse. The statue has a glaze of glassy ice upon it, from head to toe, obscuring her features, she shines gold in the morning sun, but I don't see why they let her be victimized by the weather in this way. In any case, they are all smarty-pants. Wear white. Are white. They talk about 'wondrous love' between themselves, smile like apples and wear short Wartime hairstyles. They don't believe in poverty, but in enjoying the 'wondrous fruits' of the earth—including whiskey and color television. They are, in short, very pleased with themselves, having done away with Hell, in favor of Heaven.

The peculiar thing about their worshipping the Virgin Mary is that there are no children about. Indeed, the offspring of these converts are shipped off to distant places—grandparents or dissident ex-wives. Yet the Virgin Mary was a mother first, and a Virgin second!

They all use Christian as a surname. It is a word I never admired. The man I was sent to find, Hart Christian, turns out to be the right-hand man of the invisible boss. Hart looks like Percy Bysshe Shelley. Ivy League & rich. Flaxen curls. Once he worked for the CIA, was planted in various rock concerts.

    "I don't normally do things which remind me of
    those years," he said, "but you have that despe-
    rate look which appeals to me."
I handed him the code and explained that Pedro had sent me up here. He perused it quickly.
    "This is child's play," he said.
Months, flowers, colors, money—he put the code all together

like a fancy anagram. The colors represented places on a
specific map. The letters, months. The flowers were code
names for people to contact in the places. The money was
just a matter of exchange, how much one was paid for
making a particular contact.

"Not much here for you," said Hart, "except that
yellow is the recurrent color, and yellow stands
for Cuba, that much I do know. What are you
looking for anyway?"

Just a friend, who was kidnapped by a man named Lucas.

"You're a novice, aren't you?"

He mused, twisting the Cross around his wrist, till I feared
it would stop the blood. But then he unwound it slowly.

"Does Lucas want you to work for him?"

Well, cooperate.

"Do you have any other names?"

There's a Sergeant Pepper.

He tipped his head back, revealing a remarkably soft
underchin.

"Now that's familiar. Sergeant Pepper. I never
met him, but heard the name often. No one ever
knew exactly which side he was on. But why don't
you cooperate. You'll get paid well for your ser-
vices and you can quit when you want."

No way, I said.

"You're very hostile. Now all I can advise you is
to head south, maybe even aim for Cuba."

He dropped his head and smiled up at me.

"Would you like a massage?"

No.

"You need it, you know, you have unnecessary
wrinkles around your eyes. You emulate hostility.
Suppressed rage. You need a good strong massage. We have plenty of people here equipped
to do it—"

No, thanks.

"I know your type. If I just had forty-eight
uninterrupted hours with you, you'd be a new

person. One girl just arrived the other day,
totally spaced out, a wreck, and already she's a
functioning member of the community."
What's her name?
"I don't remember. but you see, we believe that
mankind is on the verge of destroying itself. We
have the technology now to use it negatively, or to
use it positively. But people must be converted,
first, to Joy, our first principle. We call Joy the
love of Now, or step #396 on the ladder to
Supreme Wisdom."
Where does the Virgin fit in?
"She represents the creative spirit—that which
gives naturally and without corruption."
Then why don't you call yourselves Virgin instead of
Christian?
"Well, technically speaking, none of us are virgins."
Do you want to be?
"Not in a sexual sense, no. We believe in physical
love. Our people even smoke and drink as much as
they want. You don't have to give up anything to
belong to our collective. You only have to do your
share of the labor, and be open to come-what-may."
I was getting restless, but he wasn't about to stop talking.
I tried, a couple of times, to get into theology, which I
enjoy, but he said he couldn't abide dogma. It was late,
I couldn't go anywhere else, so I was stuck with this holier-
than-thou smart aleck for over an hour.
"You're still very hostile," he said again, as I
made ready to go.

Tonight I am an atheist.
The spider & the roach are the prophets Isaiah & Ezekiel.
The snow upon the land.
The boring moon.

The first word is, of course
To Eat——manger, or The Manger, masticate & nourish,
       devour, rob-from-the-landscape, transform,
       sharpen the gums, or the teeth, fill the hole with
       parts of the world, stuff the anger, engender
       energy, manipulate fleshy objects, drain, suck,
       take away some of mum, milk is to eat what
       water is to bleed—mmmmmmm

The second word is
To Sleep——dormir, dormant, schlep, do-do, dip in to
       silence, drown the brain, empty the wrists,
       multiply, rock in God, to fade away, to say
       goodbye world, to be smashed by space,
       ground under the wing of Mercury, find
       Cinderella's shoe, to sleep is to stilskin, to
       three-blind-mice, to sleep is to do the no-no

The third word is
To Want——desirer, voler, volley, dessminate, wah!,
       wampum, to lay hands upon in greed &
       yearning, to claim with the brain, to see, to go
       yo-yo-yo-yo-yo, to call aieeee when it's too late,
       to fall without wings is to want to fly, to be
       empty of, to lack & grasp at, to miss (as in je me
       manque de toi—literally: I am missing, myself,
       of you.)

The fourth word is
To Kill——kullen, cool, keel, curl, call, cull, crack-on-the-
       skull, demolish, obliterate, to call yah-yah-yah-
       yah or ach! Beautiful der killen beautifully, ugly
       der killen uglily. Mad at mama, mad at dad, mad

at someone who always had, do em in, do em out,
der gotten wormies in der snout

The last word is
To Love——lubere, amor, leaf, amiable, amazing grace,
amazon and ammunition, lamb-of-the-pink-
side, la-la,
to eat to sleep to want to kill
to want to eat to sleep to kill
to sleep to kill to want to eat
to kill to eat to sleep to want

to love equals to lug your luggage
all the way around the country
in a big blizzard
to earn some bread
to feed the one
you   is equal to

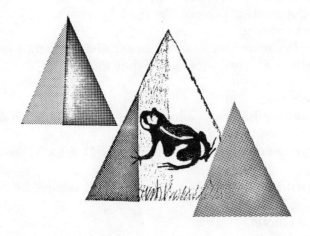

Drove south. Kept thinking Fiduciary, Fido, Fido, Fido,
till it turned into Fidelity, Infidel, Fiddle, Fidel,
Fidolatry, Fidel!

Valentine's Day as clear as a bell.
Snowballs on branches like cherryblossom time.
Everywhere I go, snow has just fallen,
A devastated landscape, cold & chunky.
Stopped in Boston and got a fake passport.
A fake State Department stamp for travel to Cuba.
Am now a slender blond.
A Florida fortune hunter.
Hearts of palm.
Washed the ashes off my brow, put on make-up & mascara.
They know everything I'm doing.
I'm making a fool of myself.
There is a hole in my stomach where love once curled secure.
I demand my daughter's return.
I asked a woman, yesterday, which way I should go.
A cleaning woman inside the Jefferson Monument.
I was crying and she said don't.
I told her my story and she said do.
We cried together.
She said go south and find my cousin Bluebell.
She'll tell you where your child is.
She's got mystical powers, she reads ice cubes.
I'm not kidding.
While they're melting in a blue saucer, she tips them around.
And she reads messages before they melt.
She's always right.
She believes.
She gave me Bluebell's address and said tell Bluebell she'd
be visiting Natchez in June.
And one last thing, my cousin is called the Dog-Faced Woman.

Am spending the night in Asheville, N.C.—home of
Thomas Wolfe.
A cheap motel.

Pink on the outside, green on the inside.
A smelly motel.
No Gideon, no television.
Cars in slush whip by in the night.
Lights flood over, are gone.
To a girlchild of six, the Vagina:
　　1. It is a flower flooded with blood
　　2. It contains Easter
　　3. It blushes
　　4. It smells of incense & myrrh
　　5. It is the middle Holy in Holy Holy Holy

　　"Sex is an appetite, just like any other," says the
　　doctor.
No, it is just the opposite.
　　"It is one of the great human expulsions? Like shit,
　　vomit, sneezes, sweat and dreams? Is this what you
　　mean?"
Exactly. You can get rid of sexual desire by various exer-
cises.
　　"Or by having sex."
Correct. Just as you have to die to overcome death.
　　"Die?! Voluntarily?!"
I do not mean suicide. Only when you die are you free of
death. As Pound suggested, it would be well if all of us
pretended we were dead already.
　　"But why?"
Courage would be natural as breathing then.
　　"Courage? for what?"
For resistance.
　　"I don't know what the hell you're talking about."
Then you're a fool.
Sleet is predicted.
I am obsessed by antlers.
Antlers antlers antlers antlers!

February 17.
I like philosophy.
It hurts.
More elephant grey, then pee-colored sky.
More snow coming.
If I can just make it over the border!
It is crucial to the natural life of the USA that I escape.
Otherwise, the groundhog won't see its shadow.
The crocuses won't bud in March.
There will be famine starvation & plague.
The weather keeps matching my moods.
Gotta get my passage confirmed.

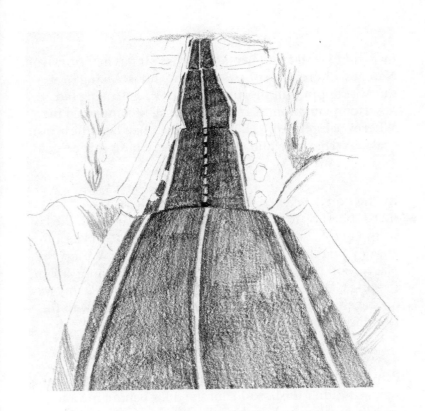

THE DOG-FACED WOMAN

I was told I could find her 'on the roof'. It was in the town of
Natchez where rows of pastel shanty houses hang over
the Mississippi. But my directions took me to a big old
deserted plantation. A frost, of course, accompanied me.
Wherever I stepped, a chill film of silver flew over the brown
grass, as wherever Midas stepped everything turned gold.

By the time I reached the door of the house, I was
surrounded by hoar-frost. The door was ajar. As in the last
scenes in *Gone With the Wind,* the interior of the mansion
was devastation. Creaking, cold, dust, cobwebs. A huge fireplace stood ruin'd and bare, but on the mantle hung a sign,
reading COME ON UP. I understood I must make my way
up the chimney to achieve my goal: an interview with the
Dog-faced Woman with her saucer of ice-cubes.

But I was scared shitless and found a bathroom under the
stairs. It didn't flush, so I shut the door behind me and
quickly approached the hearth with my purse in my hand.
Took off my wig so it wouldn't get dirty and stuck it in my
bag. I stuck my hand up the flue. It was wide and dark and
windy. There was a kind of staircase of stones, fit for a large
alley cat which I proceeded to climb, but found myself still
in touching distance of the floor, pressed against a closed
grate. I had to twist around and push at it with my back.
Slowly, it gave, rose up, and I was able to hoist myself into
more-of-the-same. This stage was Fear.

Cold to the bone and shivering. The grate slammed down

below me. Somewhere a dim chink of light was thrown in and I could glean the bare outlines of the next three stone steps, leading, again, to another flue. I scrambled upwards, fast, understanding that all of this had something to do with Death. Again, my back was my tool in pressing upwards on the flue. Again, it opened on darkness. I crawled up and felt the soft body of a rat on the first step up. The flue banged down beneath me. The rat was colder than any cold. Stiller than any stillness. The gravity of Death is great indeed. I sang aloud a song called, "Help Me God in Whom I Don't Believe.' And I skipped the step of the dead rat and lunged, backwards, for the next flue. The cold air grew more open, though the light had not intensified. I knew I must be half-way to the top and this stage must be called Hope.

My speed and agility were increasing with the repetition of the process, and I jammed up into the inevitable stage called Disappointment. Absolute darkness welcomed me. Whatever defect in the chimney's structure that had given me light before, was now lost. I was shrouded in the heavy cloak of night. A spider thumped over my wrist and swung down onto my left breast. I rushed, blindly, singing, and banged my head on the next flue. Fuck was the last word of the song.

Above the next grate, praise be to the Lord, was a great light. Far above me, then, I could see the sky. And on all sides walls without steps. The roof must've been ten feet over my head. I stood, balanced on the grate beneath me, staring up and trying to read the writing on the walls. There must be a way out. For there was no way back. That terrible moment, immortal, hit me: What if I couldn't get what I wanted? Me! Of all people!

But then it seemed that a cloud was covering the sun, for a shadow passed over me. The head of a woman was hanging

down from above. She called out, Wait! I'll drop the rope!
And drop it she did. So, like a mountain-climber, I hauled
myself upwards, palms burning, feet on the wall, till I had
arrived at the top, black as a sweep. I swung down onto the
roof where I could see my frost glittering on Spanish moss.

"You can use the fire escape going down, said
the dog-faced woman.
She wore a cloak woven with browns and yellows, her hood
almost covered her face completely. But than I saw she had
whiskers and a snout. She squatted on the sloping tiles with a
blue saucer of ice in her hands.
Your cousin, I told her politely, says she'll be coming to
see you in June.
She gave a canine growl and asked me what I wanted to
know.
"But first," she said, "you'll have to tell me the day,
the place and the weather on the day you lost it.
You have to tell me what it looks like."
"It's my daughter," I confided.
And took advantage of this notebook for such historic
details as place and weather, and I gave her the information.
She growled again and sank into a trance over her dish of ice
cubes, turning them this way and that. She wore leather
gloves. I leaned on the chimney, waiting, with my eyes shut.
It seemed many minutes before she spoke.
"I can't find her," she announced.
I started to curse but she interrupted, saying
"You must go South—then East—to speak with a
man who can help you. He has curls, black curls,
and smokes cigars. He is sitting in a wicker arm-
chair in the sun. He is as powerful as Apollo, as
mischievous as Mercury. As kind as—I don't know
who—"
I couldn't think of anyone that kind either and stared into
the distance where I could see a pale green curve—Spring—
like a Sunrise. But between myself and that greening lay a
huge expanse of ice.

"Like a pilgrim and a witch," said the Dog-Faced
Woman, "you must be, constructing cloud towers
which will fall like pillows when piled too high.
People will watch your activity with great curio-
sity, as they watch the activity of madness con-
versing, logically, with madness. They will give
names to your business, like Lost Her Marbles, but
you must ignore them. For suddenly the witch will
spring out of you, it's not for nothing that witch
rhymes with bitch, and you'll knock down your own
cloud towers before anyone else can do it, at which
point the clouds will turn to stones, curving out like
a jetty into the water, and forming a question mark,
and these will be your stones. Yours! You can name
them anything you want! Lucky woman. But if you
don't want to go through these pains, getting to the
stones, you can stay on this roof with me, rather
than face the uncertainties of your journey. We are
both miserable creatures. You can buy the food—"
I gave her some money and told her I would go, instead, to
find the curly-haired man, on the track of those stones. And
I descended the fire escape, my hand sliding on ice. For a
long time I heard her howling, as the moon would howl, if it
had a voice.

APPROPRIATE SUFFERING

There are times when we do not understand the roots
of our suffering and there are times when we do.
When we do, we experience what is called Appropriate
Suffering.
It makes sense! To suffer is reasonable, and so, to suffer

now, resembles mourning which has a time span.
The other kind, Inappropriate Suffering, can go on
indefinitely, as it is nourished by delusions.
Like physical affliction, Inappropriate Suffering leads a
person to neglect all others. Indeed, it requires constant
attention from others, and ruins everyone else's time.

Oh yeah? Suffering is absolute. You can't suffer more
or less than anyone else. So what you are saying is bullshit.

February 23. Now it's absolutely true that the weather
changed as soon as I crossed the border but not really for
the better. I woke up in the next motel, adobe, to the
sound of rain. Drumming little wet fingers. Children.
Clouds lie over the land, the sky has fallen in when it rains.
I hear that things are clearing up, North, behind me,
but I may still be dragging bad weather along. Must get
to Mexico City, fast. Cubana de Aviacion. Stamped on my
passport: Good for travel in Cuba. I am getting safe conduct
everywhere I go. Before I knock, the doors are opened.
I move like a sleepwalker through the people & the
land. Even my tires remain intact, nothing is stolen, no
one begs.

As the plane rose, the veil of rain lifted, then drifted
below us. I saw, in the end, nothing of the land below.
It was just the right sized plane, not too large, not too small.
A few bumps & trembles, silver wings flapping.
I chose to drink Southern Comfort and noted the
passengers close by me. American journalists, and some
Spanish-speaking tourists.
Yes, Cuba still has some resort hotels. Big straw hats were
flung into the overhead rocks, and baggage with floral
designs.
Briefly, I was capable of reading. This is what I read:

> The American Intelligence System resembles the
> Copernican cosmograph. It is worked out according
> to one fallacious assumption: that the Earth (Sun) re-
> volves around the U.S.A. (Earth). So just as Copernicus
> has planets missing each other by a hair's breadth,
> stars crashing and galaxies ignored for the sake of the
> original assumption, the American Intelligence has
> embargo laws, military and nuclear bases, established at
> points where they must, finally, be rejected. We honestly
> believe we are the Center, around which all revolves.
> We ignore and oppress others in order to sustain
> this fallacious faith. And we're getting away with it!

I stuffed this note away in my bag, it made me nervous, and
looked out the port hole. The sky was fulminating with spi-
rit. Clouds were delirious with joy.
The light was laughing.
And something told me, yes, even the spent moment
contributes.
You make someone happy for an hour, why bother?
It contributes.
You water your plants, why bother?
It contributes.
You help the passenger take down his case, why bother?
It contributes.
You nurse your child, why bother?
It contributes.

A good deed is a picket in the fence of your future.
Construct a magic circle, made of good deeds, around your-
self, for self-preservation, if only.
Another word is
To Fear—avoir peur, purr, pure, prune, preen, peep, peek,
           freak, free, flee, fly, flue, fluke, flop, flake,
           avoirdupois, glutton, flunky, funky and glued,
           yipes, help, attention!

There was a person on board I didn't notice at first, but
now I believe he is the one sent after me. Young, in an
inappropriate Army jacket, big hood hiding a smooth face.
I catch glimpses of girlish hips, bit it's hard to say why,
he is always hidden. Hood. Could be a college drop-out on
his way to the cane fields, but he keeps glimpsing at me
as I turn aside—almost as if he is flashing his face as
gentlemen flash their pricks in Central Park. I don't like it.
I don't like the way he keeps muttering. Who let him on
the plane, unless he is serving a function? He is staying at
my hotel, but then we all are, the journalists, the tourists.
He follows me around the hotel lobby like a dog,
whining and muttering, and only I seem to care.

Last night I had a drink, no, three, with a fat journalist who
is not suspicious. Heavy & melancholy but full of jokes. In-
stant rapport between the two of us. You can, in the end,
trust a sensuous man, especially when he has the taint
of grief about him. *Bonjour Tristesse. Hola Dolor!* He
and the other journalists are taping a story for national
television—about Cuba, about the Man himself.
　　"And what are you doing here?" he asked me.
Looking for my daughter.
　　"Some kind of runaway?"
That's right.
　　　"Children. I never had any myself, but I think
　　　you can gage from them what the judgement of
　　　God will be, upon you, in the next life. If they
　　　still come to see you, happily, when they grow
　　　up, so will God."
(I like a man who will talk about God.) But the boy in the
hood was sitting close by at another table. I noticed he wore
battered shoes & no socks. And suddenly he leaned over,
askew, so I still couldn't see his face, and asked me for
a cigarette. I gave him one, and he put his feet on a chair,
muttering and laughing.
　　"I bet he doesn't love his Mom," whispered Fatty.
What's he doing here?
　　"Don't ask me . . . Let's talk about you."
I was wearing my blond wig.
Have lost so much weight Pepsi would respect me again.
Fatty guessed I came from Tampa!
I told him I was a white Russian from San Bernardino, CA.
　　"Ah," he sighed.
Swallowed as he is, by appetite, I feel pity for him.
What does this line mean? I asked him: "Four
anguishes and one hope." I bet you don't know.
　　　"The one hope," said Fatty, "stands for the
　　　fifth step in the chain gang's march, when the
　　　slaves kicked aside the chain to make room
　　　for the four anguishes to follow."
I did not expect him to know one line of Cuban poetry,

but he has done his homework. I gave him one more test:
What did the Russians say when
they went home in 1959?
"They said, of the Cubans, Marxist-Leninist
principles were not meant to work with *these*
people in *this* climate."
And he mopped his brow and ordered us another round.

Soaked in heat, my sweat could fill a milk bottle.
It is warm, very warm.
A tropical humidity languishes, like a nun, across my bed.
So close to the Sierra Maestra!
A thick & sweet odor pervades the island reminding me of
blood.
The smell of magnolia, slavery.
I feel if I stood on tiptoes, I could predict the world.
But I'm too lazy.
The weight of gravity corresponds to the pull of despair.
I must not be deflected from my course!
On the inside of my book of poems by Nicholas Guillén was
scrawled: "Look over history, see women like flowers &
men like rocks. The one crushes, but the other is born again.
Merge elements for revolution."

February and it's hot, the starched streets of Havana
remind me of a ghost town in the Far West—yet they are
'bustling with life'. Buildings low down. The journalists
went off with two guides, I roamed the streets. Junior, as
we call him, of the Army hood, began to trail me at
a certain point, just like a little boy after his Mama. This
morning in the lobby he said something like 'then the
Germans went bang-bang-boom-boom-pow-' and he
chuckled. At least he was laughing that time. Today,
outside a bookstore, he started making whimpering sounds
that truly alarmed me. I hurried back to the hotel,

where there was a message, granting me an interview with
the curly-haired man tomorrow. I'm the only American
around here who speaks Spanish.

Fatty, who is not all *that* fat, perhaps heavy is more to the
point, and whose name is Selwyn, bought me drinks again
tonight. El Flamboyan! I had to watch it, though, because a
hangover would ruin my tomorrow. He was saying
    "It is literally impossible to be Marxist in the
    United States. Our whole mentality is geared
    elsewhere. It would be, say, like applying Tol-
    stoian principles to guests at a resort hotel in
    Puerto Rico. The guests have arrived there for
    rest, privacy and service. Correct as the manage-
    ment might be, ideologically, in asking them to
    sing for their supper, in a week he would have no
    clientele. The United States is a vacationland
    and a laboratory. A convention, endlessly. We
    use the landscape for experimentation, we don't
    seem to live there as inhabitants, in the origi-
    nal sense, but as visitors."
This was his longest statement. By and large, he murmurs
brief comments, jokey and skeptical.
You come from Westchester County, I told him.
    "Well, if I come from Westchester County," he
    replied, "you don't come from San Bernardino.
    You come from Manhattan. Why are you
    lying to me?"
What's your wife like?
    "How do you know I have one?"
You always do.
    "I told you I don't have children."
That doesn't exclude the use of a wife.
    "I did have one, but don't now."
This exchange was carried on in the highest spirits, which is
why I was able to exert enough self-control to announce my
fatigue. He stood up smiling and said:

"Go thy great way!
The Stars thou meetest
Are even as Thyself—
For what are Stars but Asterisks
To point a human Life."
I did not tell him I knew it was Emily Dickinson, for
it would show him I like a man who quotes poetry.
We all know you can speak too soon; but, as the Virgin
Mary said, you can think too soon too.

The curly-haired man sat in a wicker chair, as did I,
on a patio outside his villa. Mountains slept in the distance,
a flash of sea. Tropical flora, birdlike, appeared immortal
for the stillness of each petal. His cigar was the hour-glass
for my interview. When it was first lit, it was halfway
done, a near-stub, so I understood I didn't have much time.
He is a big man, very big, in khaki attire, hirsute as
the Dog-Faced Woman described him. Eloquent, yet
factual. He emanated patience. Caesars seize the hours,
said Mary, but this Caesar absorbs them. I did not
wear my wig to the interview (it makes my head itchy in the
heat), and he commented on my Spanish appearance, in
English, I replied in Spanish, and we were off. I started:

Q. Did you know Jaime Lopez?

He was of no use to anyone by the end. A conflict
in ideals. Sympathy for us, but need for Them.
He was, at one point, assigned to get rid of
me. It was a simple matter of charm to get him
on the plane and send him home.

Q. Do you know who killed him?

I didn't know he was killed. He will rise again, in
any case, if you get my meaning.

Q. My daughter has been kidnapped. Do you have
any idea where she might be.

In the Underworld, no doubt. Don't look for
her among the workers of the world. She will
have been swept underground to join the great
melting pot of American society, the criminals.
They are integrated down there, they boil under
the streets of your cities, they hold up the
buildings, support the structures.

Q. Did you know I was coming?

Of course. And I made inquiries in advance.
You are being protected by your enemies. But I
got the name of someone in Manhattan, someone
you can trust, here is the name and address.
I do not like to see a mother lose her child.

Q. Why not?

It makes me sick. Just like poor people make me
sick. And I don't like feeling sick.

Q. The Virgin Mary said that it's easier for a
prostitute to become a true Marxist than for a
businessman. Do you believe this too?

Of course.

Q. She also said the meek will not inherit the earth.

The definition of meek escapes me.

Q. Since it rhymes with weak, in English, we tend
to believe it has something to do with cowardice.

The French put it well. The debonnair will
inherit the Earth.

(And he rubbed out his cigar.)

"Revolutionaries must express their ideas valiantly, define
their principles and state their intentions so that no
one is deceived, neither friend nor foe."

—Fidel Castro

The Virgin whispered: "What's the profit in getting to
Heaven and leaving poor people here below?"

Below? Does this mean I am in a scheme already? Here?
Where?

If the left is always West and the right is always East, then
North must be overhead and South below. Is Canada a
metaphor for Heaven? Or close to it, and why so cold? Fire
and ice, the vertical point of the Cross. East and West,
the open arms of Nothinghood. Nottingham Forest.
Red Riding Hood.

Figure 13A.—Distribution and migration of the redstart. An example of a wide migration route, since birds of this species cross all parts of the Gulf of Mexico, or may travel from Florida to Cuba and through the Bahamas. Their route thus has an east-and-west width of more than 2,000 miles. For migration paths of greater or less extent see figures 9, 10, and 11.

> Naked feet, rocky torso,
> These from my black man;
> Pupils of antarctic glass,
> These from my white man!

"That's by Nicholas Guillèn," said Selwyn.
Then he suggested we return to the States via Canada.
We're on the same wavelength, I said.
    "I just want to see something."
If North is close to Paradise?
    "Sort of, although I doubt it," he said with his
    disarming smile.
I hear life is good in Canada.
    "I've been there many times myself," he said,
    "and at first it does seem to be a metaphor
    for Heaven. But *comme toujours*, there's a worm
    in the ointment."
A worm? In the ointment?
    "Well, let me explain."
Can I tape you?
    "Go right ahead."
We were in his hotel room and he had a very fancy
tape recorder, which had been used on Castro that same
day. He got everything ready to roll, lit up a smoke and
leaned back to speak. This is what Selwyn said:

When you cross the border, everything is French—French
birds, French trees, French restaurants, French kisses,
French toast, French people. There is a glaze of ice
(or *glace*) over the asphalt, but if you keep at it, you
reach the Palais Royale, where you always wanted to be.
In fact, it's a hotel overlooking the most lethal river in
human history: sixteen tons of ice float along its surface
daily, the banks of the river are sheer, as on the upper
Hudson. The Palais Royale is modern, clean, though a
family of roaches lives under glass (or *glace*) in a room
behind the main kitchen. You don't have to make your own

bed or sweep your own floor. The rooms are clear
as glass. At night you see the Northern Lights in the sky and
stars bursting out all over—red ones, blue ones, gold
and green ones. Your breakfast is served on a silver
tray—French toast, maple syrup, fruit juice and *café*
in a large silver pot. The children in your bed drink *café*
too, strongly diluted with milk. After their breakfast,
the children are dressed and taken off to an excellent school
where they can honestly feel that work is play. A large area
is kept green as a meadow so they can run around.
You have, in the meantime, worked at your craft or art all
day, free to take walks, pick at French fries or to converse, whenever you felt the inclination. The worm in the
ointment turns out to be that river which walls you in.
You can't cross it and you certainly don't want to cross the
border south and return to the problems you left behind.
A certain loneliness in your spacial position affects your
moods. You don't let your children, if you have them,
within one foot of the French windows the first day, then
within one and a half the second day, and so on, by
halves, until you find yourself, and them, living in bed,
waiting for service!

Imagine that, I said and switched off the tape recorder.
"I am more afraid of corruption than I am of
death," said Selwyn.
There is more corruption than death in your profession.
"In all professions," he said, "there is. But who
cares about that? The main thing is, you can't
even think straight in this world."
You sound like the Virgin Mary.
"I know I do. And I think she goes beyond
faith, in her message. That is, she implies that
faith itself is corrupt."
If you aspire to sainthood, you're setting yourself apart
from others.
"And if you, nobly, say I won't do such a thing,
you are assuming that the Creator will appreciate
your self-sacrifice and save you on the spot."
Well, then, what.
"Let's fly Air Canada tomorrow," he said.
And then?
"We'll fly from Montreal to Kennedy Airport."
We were both drinking up a storm. We felt we had
accomplished what we came for. This was a celebration.
"You will have a hangover," he said.
And you?
"I don't get them. But I have some Alka-Seltzer—
for my friends."
Kindness comes when least expected and demands
nothing in return. But as he shook out the Alka-Seltzer
for me, I felt I must express my appreciation for his
friendship. I told him I loved to fly.
Not in a jumbo jet, but in a 707, beside the window.
"Will you hold my hand? I get scared."
That was what I was going to suggest.
"You see," he said, "we're meant for each other."

ON HAPPINESS

Happiness, of which there is almost none, depends upon its fleetingness for survival. Like justice, happiness seems to be a measurable quality, but is not. But justice manifests itself madly, like a hurricane, like Watergate, it just appears and then it's gone. Happiness can be pursued by stealth and logic. But if you make the mistake of saying, Aha! Gotcha! to happiness, you can expect trouble to follow. The point is to be as quiet and cautious as possible and when you are right beside it, stop. Don't touch it. Remain in a state of underfulfillment. Breathe softly, and amorously. Cover happiness with understanding of its need to fly and see its flight before it has flown, in order to sustain an image of its stillness later. That is, don't ever expect to be happy, but only to be in the presence of happiness, as a respectful witness.

On the other hand, it is a law of Nature that whatever you recommend, or discover to be true, must be tested and found wanting. So please ignore the above, in case you hurt yourself. Don't hurt yourself, please!

"I just want you to be happy" is often the last line of a love affair. When you have stopped loving another person, you say you want them to be happy.

Remember! The most important thing is to make it home safely. That's all that counts.

Must remember: el flamboyan
                              Havana Libre
                              CLIC
                              Cuba *Libre*
                              The tobacco fields
                              Two wings of a single bird
                              Nostalgia means 'homesick'

The worst experience since Pepsi's gone. In the midst of
a deep drunken sleep, bags packed for departure, wig on
the table beside my bed, in the heat of the rising sun, I am
having a dream about the marina in San Francisco, where a
vendor is calling 'marina, marina' when I am wakened by
a hand on my face.
        Marina, Marina, says a voice.
It is Junior of the Army hood, but now I see his hood is
thrown back, and, in the golden cone of dawn, I see his face
for the first time. It's Lee Harvey Oswald.
        Shut up, he says
and brandishes a small revolver. He yanks back the sheet
and stares at my body. I wonder how he's going to do what,
with the gun in one hand, I mean, but then he throws back
the sheet with disgust.
        Only your upper lip belongs to her, he says.
He yanks my upper lip.
        I thought the whole thing was her, you.
And then he smacks me across the face, spitting out words
about Jack Ruby and Jack and Jackie Kennedy. Jack, Jack,
Jack, smack, smack, smack. My head is being tossed around,
it hurts.
        I could've spotted that lip a mile off.
I start to speak, he smacks me again, whips up his hood
and says *Dallas, my eye.* Then he is gone. I always want the
last word.

I've been framed, I said.
But who would believe this? To whom could I speak? How
explain the swollen cheek and blazing brow? I plunged my
face in cold water, swallowed four aspirin, and flopped
on the bed. The whole scene had lasted, at the most, five
minutes. Outside I could see a flock of seagulls wheeling
against the china-blue sky, their wings nearly translucent
for the whiteness. Their whines like the inarticulate whines
of small children. I stared at the patterns they made, a
blur, a Rorschach of leaves, frosted lumps of snow, when

as a Vision
the Virgin entered, winged, through the glass pane, and
threw Herself upon my bed. So! I have one more thing to
fear—I had forgotten, I thought.
>"Yes," she said, "You have one more thing
>to fear."
I recoiled, she was a human bird.
>"Remember that night," she said, "many
>years ago, when you were alone in that windy
>penitentiary? You had gone to bed, full of
>resolution, that you now had nothing to
>fear, for you had been removed from the
>human rat race. All night women moaned in
>their cots around you. But you were quiet,
>saying, I have nothing to fear. And then you
>remembered. Ghosts! The Afterlife! ESP!
>Things you feel but cannot touch! And you
>didn't sleep a wink, in terror, until the
>lantern of Heaven was lit in the East?
>Remember?"
I remembered.
She was wearing a white so white it was Blue. Her Complex-
ion was smooth and reddish brown, her Face one of those
eternal faces Lafcadio Hearn described in Mexico. A wide
Mouth, high Cheekbones, long sloe Eyes and thick blue-

black Hair. A Mayan statue. A Face that declares itself
immune to historical change, an Icon, an Emblem, a work
of Art. Untouchable.

>"Until you have lit your own lantern in the
>Eastern sector of your brain, you will always
>have fear."

How much?

>"A lot," she said, "but light that lantern, and
>stop thinking so much. You have no chance
>of glimpsing the hem of laughing light so
>long as you keep looking from left to right
>instead of, yes, straight ahead! Look straight
>ahead, plow through the cloud pillows, till
>you come upon your rocky jetty. Suck, and
>you shall be nursed. Get it?"

Then she leaned over and put her hand upon my face.
Passing her fingers across me, she healed my hangover and
my wounds in one fell swoop. I would have had it last forever. The relief she gave brought tears to my eyes.

>"Now sleep like a baby," she said, "and
>tomorrow, act like one."

Then she coalesced and flew.
I had wanted to ask her if it was true that the poor will
always be among us. Her son said so. But would she? And
could I stand it if she said yes?

We had a beautiful flight, for which I am grateful.
I felt like a glass of clear water.
My head was one pink rose.
I nourished my head.
The sweet birthday fragrance of the mature flower.
It needs clear water.
It rests its cheek on air.
It breathes.
Like a softshell clam, it opens and shuts.
Nothing offends the tribunal of water, container and air.

We had some Bloody Marys in Montreal, waiting for our flight to New York. It was here that I took a baby's leap of faith in Selwyn and told him about Lucas, Pepsi and my mission. I even told him about Oswald. I did not tell him about J, whose notes & papers I have now exhausted. And I did not tell him about the Virgin's appearance for fear it would obliterate all chances for him to make a baby's leap of faith in my direction.

"Babies can't choose their parents," he said, "but I want to live with you."

He believes me!

"I won't make any demands," he said. I told him he could live with me, but that I am a Virgin by choice for life, and I must find my daughter alone.

He agreed! We were sitting in my apartment.

"The most deadly gift one human can give
another is false hope," he said, "so I won't
even attempt to find your daughter, or pull
strings."

Thanks. But don't you have to go to work?

"No, I just free-lance. You see, I went to all
the right schools, so I have access to people
in power and I can just pick up the phone
and get the assignment I want. Call me
Lance-alot. I'm rich. Everything I have is
yours, too, so take advantage of me."

He was wearing striped pajamas and lounging on the
couch last occupied by Mr. Nobody himself. My copy of
Gorky's *Reminiscences* was on his lap. A pillow behind his
head, he picked his toes, his round fleshy face as pleasant
as a pie. The phone kept ringing, we did not answer it.

"I'll buy you a new car tomorrow," said
Selwyn, "You might as well forget the one
in Mexico City."

I have to find Sergeant Pepper tomorrow, I said.

"Just be careful. I'll wait here for you. and
I'll cook you a delicious meal."

It was late night, cold and clear outside, March, when I
went into Pepsi's room for the first time. No one had not
been in there, while I was gone. I threw his shoes out
the window.

I sneaked out early this morning, leaving Selwyn asnore on
the couch. Drenching March rain. Soggy brown. A man on
the bus said to a woman beside him, "Living badly is the best
revenge—for the children of the rich, eh?" It was a long
slow ride uptown, 102nd Street and Riverside Drive, my
destination. I had to change buses at 42nd Street, got
soaked. Vague swellings of paranoia, feeling I am watched,
a sensation like vertigo, the drag of gravity on a high
building, will I go up or down.

Sergeant Pepper. Is a woman! Immaculate, Black, slender, with that combination of warmth and reserve you get in women who have struggled to the top. Easy does it. She's probably younger than me by about five years, and much smarter. Tailored even in Levis and a checkered shirt. Short straight hair, a bony aquiline face, full lips quivering wit. Her apartment is tidy, but for the reams of newspapers lying around. A wet brown view of the Hudson.
I told her who sent me.
   "Okay," she said, "but don't tell me anything I
   don't know already."
How can I help it?
   "Just assume I know the headlines. You give me
   the small print."
My daughter has been kidnapped.
   "That's a headline."
Well, I'm not going to make any deals with anyone, I said, no organization, no individual.
   "But you want your kid back, right?"
Well, yeah!
She smiled and offered me a smoke from a silver cigarette box. She did not smoke herself, but I took one.
Who do you work for, I asked her.
   "Uh-uh," she shook her head, "That's against the
   rules."
Well, how can I trust you?
   "You got my name from a good source, didn't
   you?"
She drifted to a desk by the window. Opened a drawer and took out a letter. She gave it to me. It was addressed to me, in Pepsi's tense, jerky and hard-pressed print.

   Ma,
      I hope you're not mad at me, or getting into any
   kind of trouble on account of me. I'm okay! I got
   my period! Bad cramps but they gave me some

bufferin and Tampax. I miss you, but don't go out of
your way to find me. I'll live.

xxxxoooo

I started crying and Sgt. Pepper gave me a large man's
hankerchief with the initials J.L. sewed onto it.
"I've seen your daughter and she's just fine."
But where the fuck is she?
"You'll find out in good time."
If you were as nice as you say you are, you'd tell me. Now!
"No, I wouldn't."
Then she tugged the letter from my grasp and ripped it
into small bite-size shreds, dropping it in a basket. Very
graciously, she hustled my ass to the door.
"Come here same time tomorrow.
Alone," she said.
I tried to speak but found myself outside her door before I
could open my mouth. Have you ever walked down the
street crying?

ON PITY

Pity proceeds the deepest form of Love, and never leaves.
Pity is born in the body and is nourished in the body. Pity is
greater than consciousness, though consciousness is the
same for all and makes all one. Pity is greater than love,
proceeding and succeeding love. Pity hurts. The cup runs
over. It perceives, from inside one body, the inside of the
other body. It perceives appetite & other physical necessities.
This is all that pity perceives, nothing fancy, nothing meta-
physical or supernatural or rational. But without pity,
there can be no lasting, no charitable love. There can be no

hope, no faith. The expression of pity is grief. As Emily
Dickenson wrote to Mrs. Hills: "When Jesus tells us about
his Father, we distrust him. When he shows us his Home,
we turn away, but when he confides to us that he is
'acquainted with Grief', we listen, for that also is an
Acquaintance of our own."

I told Selwyn nothing of what transpired. He was making
lunch, in my apron, for us, with groceries he had bought
while I was gone. I could hardly look at him, till I was
drunk. Then I got so drunk I could hardly see him anyway.
It was a late lunch, a long lunch, consisting of coquilles
St. Jacques, onion soup, French bread, brie, camembert and
salad. The rain was hammering at the glass panes through-
out the afternoon. A gurgle in the background. We played
some music, Charlie Parker & Yusef Lateef. Perhaps
because I told him nothing of what transpired with Sgt.
Pepper, we developed a rare, nearly speechless rapport. Like
two big cats moving around an empty house on a rainy day,
licking our paws and whiskers. Nothing much to say, but
occasional lengthy stares at one another, placid or piercing.
The dread of loving makes me sick (I just threw up) and
the dread of J returning at any moment. A woman in my
old shoes has two choices: to pursue amour where she
finds it, or to walk the other way as soon as she spots it coming.
The latter produces wonderful results, the former nasty.
If Selwyn would just stay in my vicinity, but nearly invisible,
guardian, benefactor, object of abstract & uncrushed
longing, dropping me notes, writing me letters,
recommending books, why not?

Sensual passion, springing from friendship, feels like
an antler.

Alone, again.
It might as well be spring.
But it might go cold again, too.
A white crocus.
It's seven p.m.
The North Vietnamese are winning.
I'm out in a country house, but don't know where.
Was brought here, by Sgt. Pepper, in a snappy little red Toyota.
She wrapped a kerchief around my eyes and off we went.
Two hours of blindness.
I could judge time by the radio.
We talked about schools in New York City, racism,
gardening and inflation.

Then we bumped down a hill and I was revealed to midday
gloom.
A brown house in a sunken area.
The sound of a train not too far off.
My hangover didn't help me deal with the experience.
She gave me some aspirin and some valium out of her purse.
A summer house, damp but orderly, four bedrooms.

She kept her jacket on, got logs from the back steps and
built a nice fire from old newspapers.
      "Relax," she said.
But how long will I be here?
      "Can't say. Maybe one, two days."
My daughter?
      "I don't know yet. I'm going to town to get
      some food. Take care of your head."
I sat in front of the fire to wait for her return.
I was scared, lonesome.
No one would know where I was.
She came back and we ate sandwiches. Then she left, saying
she'd be back in the morning.

They arrived with the sun—a carload of individuals with
cases. Brief cases. Pepper was among them. She carried
groceries, and booze. Flashed a glance at me, laden with
good will, even comraderie. Then nothing but cold radiance.
I had had a good sleep, dunked in valium, it left a calm
place in me. My first impression of the three men was that
they were all exactly alike—as lumps of granite appear the
same, or three German shepherds on a street corner. Sloping
shoulders, flat pale faces, slick black hair, poor textures to
clothing and skin.

For a time, they murmured among themselves, while I
helped Pepper put groceries away. I felt quite at home then.
A tactical error, perhaps, on their part, or one she might

have constructed, leaving me in the house, alone, for several hours. I was the woman of the house at a subconscious level. They had come to visit me on my territory. They were bickering in soft tones, I understood that they were terribly stupid, that Pepper is the brain, the bullet, the spear, the gut, the tough nut to crack. Then things began to happen.

I was put in an empty bedroom, was told to wait. I sharpened the pencil in my brain, preparing to transcribe what occurred. And in came the first of them—Mister Poole. He introduced himself, pleasantly enough, but did not sit down beside me on the bed. He stood by the door and began to speak, all in a rush, as if he had switched a tape recorder on, under his tongue. Mister Poole:

"You think you're so smart. You think you've got all the answers. You talk a big game, about politics and history, you've got a big mouth. But you never do anything. You're conservative to the core. Basically, you're only interested in Number One. And meanwhile, the world is going to hell. But you aren't going to do anything about that, but talk. A familiar type, you are. I'd like to kick you from here to Broadway, arrogant bitch. I know all about you. But I've been told to intimidate you, not terrorize you, which is my usual job, and I'm good at it. So I'll intimidate you. I'll remind you of the mess you made fifteen years ago, running around with some ass-hole dude, who couldn't even pull off a clean robbery, and you didn't even have the guts, then, to go along with him, you talk a big game, but given the chance to really perform, you back out. There's a place reserved in Hell for people like you, the do-nothings, so why should I waste my time on you in this world? Why? Because I don't believe in an after-life, not heaven or hell, I believe in Now. And if you could just face where your real allies are, you could do something. Your daughter. She's waiting for you, she wants her Mommy. But how did she get where she is? Because of that same Mommy's ego. You never needed to lose her, and you sure as hell could've had her home a long time ago. Face it, bitch, it's all your fault. We've come all this way, and we're damn busy men, to get you to act. For the first time in your life. If you don't, you won't see the kid again. We've had lots of them like her, it won't be nothing new. Black and White and Red all over— that's what we call people like you, downtown—but then, you're just a big mouth, a talker, and who, in a dog's age, can respect that."

He shook his finger at me, but it wasn't a finger, it was a knife, and turned around and left.

I waited for a long time for the next one, I went over and over what Mr. Poole said, till I couldn't forget it.

The second man did not wear a collar, but was called The
Right Reverend Canon Brooke. Must be Episcopal, I
thought. His mouth was less tense than the other guy's, in
fact it was slack and wet. His skin was not as blotchy. (I was
beginning to perceive small differences between them.) He
too hung by the door. When his voice emerged, it was
nasal, goosey, Episcopalian all the way. The Right Reverend
Canon Brooke:

> "This is not a position I enjoy, but then, I can only pray
> I have it in my power to prevent unnecessary suffering.
> Yes, that really is my desire—to see you reunited with
> your daughter. I have no political alliances, so you can
> be sure I am speaking only for myself, when I beg you
> to summon up all the resources of motherhood and
> rush to protect your young one. She cries for you, she
> needs you. You must not think of yourself any longer.
> Obey the authority of Love and remember that the
> best slaves were always the closest to God, the holiest
> of people. By perfect obedience to an authority
> outside yourself, you will slip through the needle's eye
> into Paradise. You think too much of yourself. We all
> do—sometimes more, sometimes less—but now, under
> these extraordinary circumstances, go where Love
> leads you—to your one and only child. I can assure
> you, you will be rewarded."

He batted his eyelashes at me, and left, softly. Wool, wool!

Now the third man was the most highly trained, I believe,
and he appeared more confident than the others. Not too
aggressive, not too withdrawn. Right in the middle. He
had a deep line between his brows, which the others had not,
and a small intellectual pucker to his lips. I was not
surprised, then, when he announced himself as Doctor
Water. Ph.d.

"Let me say at the outset: I am a psychologist. Don't let this frighten you, please. I am sure by now you imagine you are having paranoid fantasies that all of us, in this house, are here as symbols rather than real people. That must be very frightening indeed. I understand you have a tendency to paranoia anyway, and, as we all know, it is a difficult illness to treat, since one's fears are usually justified at frequent intervals. But, believe me, we are real people, not offsprings of your imagination, and we all live real lives outside of our work. I want you to know this because, as I say, I know quite a bit about you. Alcoholic parents who blew their brains out in a mutual suicide pact or in the midst of a violent scene. You grew up in a mobile home, travelled continuously as a child. Ran away with a professional gambler when you were sixteen. Worked in various casinos, in the Southwest, until you ran into the fellow who got you pregnant. Etcetera, etcetera, etcetera! Well, all that just to indicate my knowledge of your history. It appears that you like to play a maternal role to would-be revolutionaries, drifters. You have a good deal of repressed anger and some fuzzy ideas about right and wrong. You transfer your personal frustration into political attitudes, but remain unable to assert yourself—politically—and drink too much to compensate. You belittle yourself, do just enough work to pay the bills, but do not aspire towards anything better for yourself. Instead, you bury yourself in books, not serious books which deal with the facts, but in fantasy—fiction, poetry—which do not rock the boat. You are sexually frustrated, having lived alone for so long, and harbor multiple resentments against good-looking women and sensual men. So you stick around failures, drop-outs, people who can't threaten your weak self-image. Now, you have lost the only relationship which confirmed your femininity, your conventionality, your stability. Your daughter has been the one link between yourself and society, and you have allowed that link to be severed. If you have one shred of self-respect left, you will lift yourself out of your inertia and act. You have the chance, it is here now. All you have to do is say yes. For your benefit, as well as for hers."

He left. I stared out the window into the woods. Straight trees, brown, devoid of leaves. All the leaves were old ones, on the ground. Bleak. Must be Connecticut.

I flew the coop.
Through the window.
been running all afternoon.
Into the night, the North Star behind me, over marshes, dry
fields, through brush, through briar, whiplash branches,
fern and graveyard. My bag banging at my side.

> North
> North by East
> Northeast by North
> Northeast by East
> East by North
> East
> East by South
> Southeast by East
> Southeast by South
> South
> South by West
> Southwest by South
> Southwest by West
> West by South
> West
> West by North
> Northwest by West
> Northwest by North
> North by West

A helicopter buzzed over, two trains passed by, lights
ablaze like crocodile eyes, horrendous noise,
and finally, maybe six miles later, I came to a depot
beside the tracks and the depot was near a little motel. This
little motel. I must've been running for hours. It was
only seven p.m. But my face was steaming. A solicitous little
woman took me to a room with a shower. I stood under
hot water for a long time, trying to rinse away the great
yellow trail of guilt & error under my feet. Where I stand, it
lies, waiting for me to take the next false step. So I stood
still, after so much running, but it didn't wash away.
There was a diner down the road. And a liquor store. I got

a plate of fish 'n chips to go, and a pint of whiskey. Looked
all around and around for those three little men. If you
twirl any object around fast enough, it makes a circle.

Last night
I was polishing off the whiskey and watching Barney Miller
on the tube, when there was a knock on the door. It was a
special knock. A knock I know, it knocked the wind right
out of me! I went to the door and said okay.
        "James," he said.
Alone?
        "Alone."
I opened the door and he was there, alone, dressed like a
gaucho in tan-colored clothes, boots and a broad-rimmed
black hat. He grasped my wrist.
    "I'm in a hurry and can't come in."
What do you want then?
    "You've lost weight."
He leaned on the door jam in his particular way, grinning,
and I leaned beside him in mine.
    "That galloping gourmet has got to go,"
    he said.
You mean Selwyn?
    "Right. Either you get rid of him, or they will."
Just let them try it.
    "I'm talking about me. Understand? I want
    him out of your life, and mine, now."
I'll think about it.
    "You think too much. If you weren't so lazy,
    you'd be dangerous."
Motherfucker.
    "See you."
Then he winked and sauntered away. There was a florist
truck, waiting for him, the engine idling, he got in and

night folded over him. Signed, sealed and delivered. And
the memory lingers on. The weakening defense system.
The collapse of Saigon.

My first visitor in prison was Mary. And she only came that
one time. I was suffering inconsolably from claustro-
phobia. Obsessed by suicide as my only hope for escape,
I had been put in solitary, on heavy drugs, all my belongings
removed from me. Around me the prison bars and walls,
the rituals, the restrictions; inside me, memories of freedom—being able to come and go as I chose, of being able to
eat what I liked, to smoke, drink, talk, read. And most
importantly being able to hug my child and inhale the
fragrance of her youth—All gone! I was, overnight, under
the yoke of the State. I was an object, owned, demoralized,
bullied. Nothing worse can happen to no one!
I had been working for ILGWU ("Look out for the Union
label!") and considered myself free.
I had been caring for man and child, and considered myself
free.
I *was* free.
I could still get up and walk out the door.
But no more.
Serving Time. Handmaiden to Hours.
Then, one dawn, in solitary, or The Hole, she came to me
like a geometrical equation, a detail on the wall:

It meant: "Even if you o.d., you will live. Forever. There is no escape, even through suicide. So relax and enjoy it and be good."

Last night I dreamed I had the name Anon again. I was something of a poet, but a naked poet who could not go out on the streets. No clothes, no way to get them. So I prowled around, like an animal in a cage, and each window had a different view. One a city, one a meadow, one an ocean, one a cloud-spangled sky. Finally, it occurred to me to wrap a curtain around my body, and then it occurred to me to go to the FBI. So I wrapped a yellow curtain around my body and, in a flash, found myself in a huge shiney room full of files and typewriters, empty desks. This

was the FBI. They would tell me what was the crime
that had brought me to this naked state. Once I understood
what the crime was, I would be able to forgive myself,
and, having forgiven myself, I would be clothed and
famous. A man appeared, a soft-spoken gentleman, who
pulled out my file and I heard myself crying at birth.
He ran through the file which chattered like a sped-up
tape, then he threw it down at my feet. He said, *There is no
crime but this: Lives like yours just take up space.*

Archie Bunker said: "Why should I work my ass off for
twenty years, just to get equality in the end?"

Selwyn was still at my place, though two days had passed.
He had, of course, been in and out, had gotten himself clean
clothes, books, had been to his office, shaved. I arrived
mid-morning.
        "You look diseased," he said.
Did anybody call?
        "The phone was ringing but I didn't answer it."
I took a hot bath, muscular tics in my calve, nerves.
He talked to me through the locked door.
        "Why won't you tell me what happened?"
It's a secret!
        "But how can I help you?"
Scram, Bozo, that's how.
        "Don't say that," he laughed. "It hurts my
        feelings."
I hate feelings.
        "You're just in a bad mood. I'll wait it out."
I heard him shuffle off. If you are absorbed by the presence
of Unexpected Kindness, you must rise, like water, to its
level.

I sat up.
Hey, come back, I didn't mean it.
I heard him shuffle back to the door.
　　　"What can I do to help?"
Just stick around, but don't ask me questions.
　　　"I promise," he said, "and now I'll go make
　　　lunch."
Go light on the garlic, I shouted.

We were sitting in the livingroom, sipping our way through
a bottle of Bristol Cream, when we heard a rattle and
a splat in the hall. It was a letter, slipped under the door.

　　Cherie:
　　　We are cruising around outside. Les jeux
　　sont faits. A plane will be waiting at New Haven
　　airport to transport you to French Canada.
　　Province de Quebec. La Belle Province! You
　　will see Sgt. Poivre who will be accompanied by
　　your petite fille. Together, you 3 femmes will
　　travel est to Saint-Henri where you will meet a
　　man in a little chalet by a highwater river. He will
　　conclude your problèmes. Bring ton passport.
　　Be in New Haven, toute suit. 5:30 A.M.
　　　　　　　　　　　　　　　—Les Trois Rivières

　　P.S.　No journalists allowed!

"There must be a post office in Saint-Henri,"
said Selwyn, "I'll meet you there the day
after your arrival. At ten a.m. If you don't
show up, I'll find you."

I told you to stay out of it, I said.
He went into the kitchen and produced a tray of food &
coffee. I looked out the window to see if I could see the
culprits, but saw nothing significant. Déjà vu! Every day
begins to read like a blueprint of another. Like biting a fruit
to remember the taste. Memory, memory. There depends
on Here, but Here should not depend on There.
   "Who is this character James," asked Selwyn.
What character James?
    "The one who is all around this house. What
    was your relationship with him?"
Was, is.
   "Is what?"
If he was my daughter's father, he may now be her lover.
I've know them both for about the same amount of time, so
it would be natural.
   "Ah," he sighed.
Then he produced a piece of paper, signed James the
Original, which had been rolled up inside the toilet paper.

I. THE AMERICAN

I am an American because I was born here. Home is home,
as an orange comes from an orange tree and a fig comes
from a fig tree. I am an American product. I know it best
when I am in exile. To be depressed in exile is to be very
depressed indeed, even if you despise your own country.
And what I hate about America is that I must ask for attention as long as I am here. The mark of a failure in America
is being ignored. And to be ignored you must have no
ambition, be blind to the riches around you. It puts a

terrible strain on a person to always be needing attention. I am tired or it! I travel to a poor country and feel panic & wonder, because everyone around me is getting along without me and my American attitudes. The goals are simple, food on the table, healthy children, a bed under a roof. But I am corrupted at source. An ego-maniac like all my people. I want fame more than I even want food! If I really wanted to contribute to the destruction of my country, I would have to do all but die. Go on Welfare. Settle for food on the table. Become passive, and even attempt humility. And that, of course, would be an act too. Even a recluse is showing off in America!

"This is an interesting document," says Selwyn.
You shouldn't have read it.
"I couldn't help it. Besides, it's too late to
talk about should and should not. Our
slogans have turned into our vows."
I stared at him with a moment's poignant suspicion, but then relaxed.
Okay, then, I told him, you can meet me in Saint-Henri.
We had hours to kill before my departure. What to do. I went into Pepsi's room and packed some of her clothes in a bag. One of her old Barbi dolls was lying in a drawer with its legs up and its hands under its head, blond hair spread out wild, eyes closed.
I hope the kid is still a virgin, I told Selwyn.
"Like yourself?"
Right. She better be.
"How do you punish a fourteen-year old girl?"
With the back of the hand applied to the front of her face.
"You mean it still works?"
If she wanted to be stroked instead, it works. Besides, the Virgin Mary Herself said slap the other cheek if it offends you.

How else do you think she stayed a virgin? And how else do
you think Jesus learned to be so good?
"But he tipped over all those tables."
He was drunk.
We sat in the livingroom reading for a couple of hours
before we started to drink. The couple that reads together
may stay together. But the couple that drinks together
has a bond that surpasseth human understanding.

"Oneida," he said, "was your father Iroquois?"
No, well, my mother was a Seneca.
"And your father?"
French Canadian. He worked in the mills, we lived in a
trailer, south of the Canadian border. I was the only child
after the other two died. They drank a lot, maybe too much.
'I'm just a bottle floating on the sea of life,' my father would
roar. They were popular in bars. Yes, I'm sure it was
suicide, for even in their deepest drunks, they always made
it home safely. But I wasn't there to be sure.

ONEIDA: a member of an Iroquoian people whose
language was noted for its complex system of
verbs.

a rock which someone set up and which is still
standing near some ancient village.

a community of perfectionists which held that sin
can be eliminated through social reform.

a lake in central New York State—20 mi. long,
5 mi. wide.

a joint-stock company organized in 1881.

"One way to achieve social justice without
violence," suggested Selwyn, "would be if
rich people like me were forced to marry
poor people like you."
A merger of separate interests. What would you get out of
it?
"Freedom from guilt—and you."
He kissed both of my cheeks, European-style, before I took
off for the airport.
Am I cooperating with them, or am I still free? I asked.
"You haven't given them what they want,"
he said, "so let's assume you're still free,
and they've given up."
That sounds fishy.
"What's the alternative?"

It was the smallest airplane ever made. Surely a toy. A yellow
toy. Like my dream curtain. Two seats for pilots. Two
seats for me and my bag. The sun was rising in blinding
hues, like pansies or oil on a clear sea. Baby clouds, flat-
bottomed, skudded by. Once I went up to an observatory
tower and saw the rings around Saturn close up. They
hurt me, don't know why, but the horror of their reality was,
like a miracle, heart-breaking. Some chunks of snow lay

on the ground below, the more North we flew. Pine and slashes of ocean. I seriously assented to Fate. I was alone, in the sky, with a stranger.

The back of his head was hidden by a helmet. Cerberus!!? And there was something of the dog in his hairy hands on the wheel. I am not a woman who likes to cry, and the entire time in transit was spent warding off tears. I had no reason to trust these people. My daughter might not be there at all, but a pair of scissors waiting to snip off my eyes. Shears for my ears. A scythe for my neck.

We stopped twice to refuel. Cowabunga! The front of the pilot's head was concealed by a plate of dark plastic, attached to the helmet, he did not speak to me. It must have been around nine in the morning when we reached our destination. A small airfield, a concrete building, signs in French. I climbed down the rope ladder, clumsily, looking for Pepsi. But there was no one around, not even customs. I followed the plump pilot. There was a black car waiting, one man at the wheel, one in back. Together they formed the three little men from the brown house in Connecticut—the pilot revealed himself as the first one, the mean one. The driver was the shrink, and I was shoved in back beside the Right Reverend! He cast his arm over my shoulders, and I sank my teeth into the fat part of his thumb.
　　　"Ow!"
　　　"Cool it," said the mean man.
The Right Reverend blew on his thumb, supposedly to 'cool it', then stuck it in his mouth and sucked on it, first for the pain of my bite, then, let's face it, for pleasure.

Outside the window—brick and concrete houses, distant pining mountains, the clear sky. Morning is the next best thing to being in Heaven. I thought I saw the Virgin waving from on high. Little gauzy buds, like the discarded nightgowns of elfin nightlife, were draped from the tips

of the branches—Spring was coming, filmy and green.
We drove up winding highways into the mountains, and I
caught a view of the Saint Lawrence River, wide as the
Hudson, and of the grey city of Quebec. I bit my lip and
swore I would not think of Pepsi, or of Happiness, till
it was over and gone, the moment, if it should ever come.

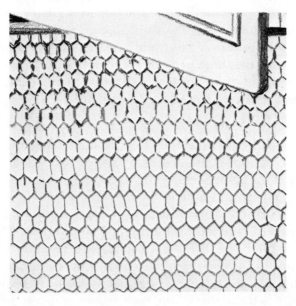

Knock and the door will fall down on you, said the Virgin,
Sneak and you shall find.

So I asked the men no questions, and sat still as a rock
deposited by human hands.

"Did you think about what we said to you?"
asked the driver out of the blue.
I dreamed about it, Doc, but I didn't have time to think.
"You shouldn't have run away like that. We
lost a lot of time tracking you down. Two days."
This remark of his assured me that J was not part of this
conspiracy, and it gave me a moment's pleasure, as the
bird puffs out its chest and whistles, I sighed.
"Do you exercise?" the shrink continued.

I do. I swim at the Y and play a mean game of squash.
       "Ah, more aggressive traits!"
He was slipping. Even the best constructed ladder has a
beginning and an end. We swooped off the highway,
bearing right down a hill. A narrow silver river on the left,
West, and a meadow on the right, East. The Reverend
took his thumb out of his mouth, wiped it dry on his pants
and looked woefully in my direction. We were reaching
the end of the journey. Apprehension fled and I felt,
instead, depression coming. At the bottom of the hill was a
small red cabin, on stilts, facing the water. The car
stopped. All the men turned to look at me.
       "Okay, get out, bitch," the mean one said.
       "We're leaving," said the shrink.

I got out and stood back while their car made a U-turn and
chugged away up the hill. A froth of dust. A scarlet
tanager sang in a tree. I started slowly towards the house,
watching the windows and doors. Screens prevented my
seeing inside. The sun was hot, the sky clear. A small
wooden porch that sagged. Two chairs. I started up the
steps, and entered. The sun in my eyes was spotty. But
I sensed a presense I couldn't see. A dark, damp little place.

A kitchen, a livingroom with a round table, four chairs,
and a couple of old armchairs facing a fireplace, still warm,
and gleams of sparks shot from the ashes. Wood stacked
beside it. My eyes cleared. I saw Pepsi's hat on a chair,
picked it up and walked to a door. An empty bedroom.
Another door. An empty bathroom. Into the kitchen,
where a birthday cake was sitting on the table. It read
HAPPY BIRTHDAY MA. One candle. There was
coffee on the black stove.

I didn't dare use my voice.
I sat down in front of the birthday cake.
My tears fell on Pepsi's hat.

Bushed & ambushed.

There was a note in the inside rim of Pepsi's hat, and it only said, "Sorry, but you'll just have to be patient."

I stood up and saw the Virgin Mary leaning near the fireplace. She was stoking it into flames with her toe. I went and stood beside her.

  "She says she's sorry," I said, "and she better be
  sorry. Very sorry. She's just like her father,
  always elusive."
Those who are quick to apologize are quick to repeat the offense, said the Virgin.

  "And why the birthday cake?"
You were born in this hovel, she said, then added: "It is easier for a mother to find a needle in a haystack than for a virgin to ride a camel."

Then she went up in smoke.

Geography abounds. Tubby buds on crooked stems, pine & birch. Is this Siberia? Is it ever. The round world, the girdle expands in the middle, swelling for pleasure, the Sun. Here I am near the top, the pate, the plate. The United States lie below me, grographically speaking. My

birthday, May, I have just passed over the peak of my
life's cycle, I can feel it in my bones. Because the voices of
childhood are calling me, because I feel memory as a
magnet drawing me home. I have no guide, but the
voice of the Virgin, now growing weak and confused. She is
beginning to babble. Every adventure ends as a story.
Every person wants to go home. Mother!

The river carried logs downstream, timber cut in the distant
mountains, sent spinning on water, some get lodged in
twigs and mud and stone along the shore. But most roll on.
I like to watch them. Orchards still crumpled and forlorn.
Dried-up ochre sheaves of grass. Redwinged blackbirds.

For a long time Home is only where you sleep. Then it is
where you get your messages too. But after a certain
birthday Home is a whole society, fulminating with voices
from the Dead, the familiar voices blending into
birdsongs on your windowsill at dawn. Comforted by the
tracks of those who have gone ahead of you, your limits
extend after them. You are alive but part of you is underground already. When whom you love or have loved dies,
part of you goes too, and you are picked apart, gradually,
piece by piece, until oblivion is as natural as sleep.

A long day, a long evening, alone, the sky at twilight immense
& wonderful. Gold versus silver. Like the reins & bits of
circus horses, shining with spittle & sweat, it goes round
and round, like circus bells, like circus ropes, the filtering
silver dust like pollen, through the long pines & the crowds
of birds applauding, lacklustre, but luminous, doomed &
blue, tent, carousel, ballon & every other banality, but true.

No smoke, no drink, but sleep.
A clear morning—minty voices from the birds.
Coffee & old birthday cake.
The Virgin said, Blessed are the bores,
for they are always nice.

And added: But being boring is a sin.

So which is more important—being sinful or being nice?

Important to whom?

To God.

What God? What the hell are you talking about? God?!

Selwyn arrived, on foot, having hitch-hiked from the p.o.
mid-afternoon. He looked mighty scared, but, boy, was I
glad to see him. Now he is sitting at the window with
binoculars, bird-watching, he says, but I know he expects a
tribe of maniacs to attack us.
      I never expected you to come, I told him.
      I feel at home with you, he said.
      Don't say that, I warned him
for I knew it was, literally, a fatal remark.

Exile is a form of suicide. Social suicide.
It's resurrection from the dead.

You have to go home.
Home is internal or one other person.
Home is society, you have to participate and clean it up.
Sometimes you clean it up by leaving.
Only if you think you are part of the problem.
I only know about three out of a thousand people who
actually improve things by staying. And they are not the
bitter, the dissatisfied, the angry or the poor. They are
happy, productive, optimistic and well-fed.

Selwyn picks his toes, rubs the grime between his thumb
and forefinger. When he leans down, his face bulges
with veins. He is sweating sickle-stains around his arms and
back. He breathes heavily. He wants us to live happily
ever after in the Canadian wilderness. The antlers of the
young deer are bloody & sore.

I left the bed at midnight and went onto the sagging porch.
Selwyn was snoring pitiably indoors. He had brought a
quart of Canadian Club which I took a little of, but
still no cigarettes. What stars!—stars, stars and more stars!

      "It is beautiful, isn't it," said a voice from the
      darkness.
He stood at a distance, his dark gold body draped in white,
the white water rushed down behind him.
You again! I sobbed.
      "Say I am your one and only," he said.
You are, you are.
      "Then why am I jealous?"
He's just taking care of me.
      "No. I am."
You're not doing a very good job of it.
      "That's what you think. I haven't let the kid

out of my sight since they ran off with her."
Is she all right?
      "She's all right."
And what about you?
      "I walked all the way up the Hudson across
      Lake Champlain. Now I'm broke and
      have to get a gig somewhere, just to tide me
      over."
When will I see you again?
      "You will, don't worry."
But when?
      "Remember, I know these parts as well,
      if not better, than you."
I remember.
      "Please dispose of this fat honcho."
I can't, he's nice.
      "But we love each other!"
He began to approach, softly as if on snow, and I went forth
to meet him, when Selwyn called my name. My edges
burned away.

Let's go for a walk, I said today.
      "I'm lazy," Selwyn protested.
So am I, but let's go!
So he came with me, reluctantly. I knew he was really afraid,
who could blame him. Where the grass is green, it shines,
each blade captive of sunshine. Colorful episodes—a
yellow fiddlehead, a cluster of dandelions, some blue
myrtle, small brown pinecones the size of Far Eastern
roaches curled in the soft dust. The water rushing ice cold
down from above. White curls of birch. The sun seemed
to penetrate me through thick layers of flesh, in a string,
an optomotrist's light in a dark room, a needle, so
thin and frail. We crushed along. A path very narrow
borders the river. A smell of burning leaves indicates the
presence of more human life in the vicinity. It's a lovely
smell, youth and fall. Selwyn panting at my side.

We sat down so he could recover on a grassy knoll. A
mountain's shadow as square as a schoolbook depository
building. The water sounds like a row of cars passing. I feel
the eye of the sniper in every tree. We had one of those
rare communications, then, without words, our brains
appeared to converse in some supernatural sense,
perfect balance, where he lounged fat in a white shirt
beside me. Or was I communicating with myself, I wondered.
No! He said, *I'm my own Grandpaw,* and it was just what
I was thinking. Really, he smiled. Then there was a
smack—like a doctor's hand on a baby's bottom—
and Selwyn fell—his head in my lap—all blood—dead.

Don't ask me no questions, I'll tell you no lies.
Been walking for hours.
Say, you sit like a Buddha under a tree.
Or cultivate your own garden.
Say, you know at every moment that what's good for you is
bad for someone else, so you better let the bad come
on your head instead. Say, you live by this, renouncing the
love of you life, your child your home your sweetheart,
because your presence elsewhere will make life better for
them.
Say, you fight for nothing, hold onto nothing.
You live alone.
You eat cabbage & bread.
You have a couple of little vices which tide you over.
You fall in love with Nature, who has been your most
constant companion all along, and babble with yourself.
You bother no one.
You scratch pictures of antlers on pieces of paper.
You grow smaller & smaller until you are elfin.
And then there really are giants, the Biggies, the Rich Folk,
the Pros, the Meanies.
You know they are the owners of the Earth.

They are just doing what God told them to do.
But not you.
You are after wisdom and it's crushing.
You sit at your little table, with your one little chair and one
little plate and tiny utensils, scrutinizing minutia.
You are humble by day.
You hide away from the giants, petrified.
And only at night are you victorious.
Night is your time, when you are phosphorescent and fly,
when you are magic and spark, when no one can see you.
You are rocked in the bosom of Blackness.
Of Dew of Owl of Perfumes of Anonymous
Obliterating Enchantment.
Dreams! Fantasy! More delicious than all the
wines of France.
Another nocturnal episode—and you are gay again!
Say, this is all your soul requires.
And every day you grow smaller & smaller.
Until you are invisible even to yourself.

Oh Selwyn! by now the flies will be eating your face!

I remember you quoting from Keats:

> When I am through the old oak forest gone
> Let me not wander in a barren dream
> But when I am consumed with the Fire
> Give me new Phoenix-wings to fly at my desire.

But pain is the thing without wings.

You should hear the questions the children ask me!
Is there water on the moon?
Does the Sea of Desolation splash in light?
How do you make the color Red?
Here is a statue in gold of Jesus and His Mother.
Here is une elise still patched with dirty snow.
Great cliffs fall to the mighty St. Lawrence.
Oil tankers, oil drums.
Drums of the Huron Indians echo on aluminum:
>   "Father, take pity on us," said the Ottawa
>   orator, "for we are like dead men."
>   Convers returned, "If you say that again,
>   you are a dead man."
>   "It is well," replied the Rat.

Dwarf houses & French things.
Now it is spring.
Then it will be summer.
In August it will begin to cool for the long winter.
Smoke among the trees.
A cold climate is not suitable for the poor.
The slaves themselves returned across the Border South.
The Great Slave Lake is a resort.
Trudge, trudge.
The buds grow fatter hourly.
Stars emerging at each branch tip, painted toenails on a child.

Passed what appeared to be an Army base.
Khaki trucks, barrack housing, children played in trim grass.
A helicopter watched me from above.
Remember Ho Chih Minh!
It's natural to follow a river,
To move by night with the North Star your compass.
And rest by day in the sun.
Such good weather, such generosity.

I understand that there is no reason for it, and why.

If only I were small, a jackrabbit, a sparrow!
Lost love—but your capacity for loving grows with time—
Crisp lilacs baking in the June sun.
Crushed purples & the fragrance, moist as a lover's breath.
Death whirls around me, Disney bluebirds following Bambi.

"I hate nostalgia. It's the American disease."
That's what the woman said. What woman? Someone trying
for brutal effect. Who said it? I must remember who
said it, for the statement keeps coming into my head, and it
makes me mad! Mad! Nostalgia is exhalation,
homesickness, sigh, pneuma, passage of breath to Breath.
I don't remember who said it, I hate ideas.

But if I follow this river Southeast?
Smell of burning, European.
Converted my money to Canadian.
I remember who said it.

Curious patterns in the scrub, purples, a spot of yellow,
a spray of forsythia. The carpet of the Underworld woven
on the surface of space.

Than I saw my rocky jetty, shaped like a question mark.
It jutted off a black beach into the sea. It was part of a photo
hanging in a diner. The rest of the photo were children.
"Where is that place?" I asked the children's mother.
"*Sud-est,*" she said.
"*Loin d' ici?*"
"*Vingt kilos, peut-être.*"
"*Ah bien.*" And I was off & running.

THE MOTHERS OF CANADA

"After the regiment of
Carignan was disbanded,
ships were sent out
freighted with girls
of indifferent virtue,
under the direction of
a few pious old duennas,
who divided them into
three classes. These
vestals were, so to
speak, piled one on
the other in three dif-
ferent halls, where the
bridegrooms chose their
brides as a butcher
chooses his sheep out
of the midst of the
flock...The marriage
was concluded forthwith,
with the help of a priest
and a motary; and the
next day the governor-
general caused the couple
to be presented with an
ox, a cow, a pair of
swine, a pair of fowls,
two barrels of salted
meat, and eleven crowns
in money."

---La Hontan

THE FATHERS OF CANADA

"Une foule d'aventuriers,
ramassés au hazard en
France, presque tous de
la lie du peuple, la
plupart oberés de dettes
ou chargés de crimes."

--Mere Marie de l'Incarnation

THE COUNCIL OF THE IROQUOIS

"It is a greasy assemblage,
sitting sur leur derriere,
crouched like apes, their
knees as high as their ears,
or lying, some on their
bellies, some on their backs,
each with a pipe in his
mouth, discussing affairs of
state with as much coolness
and gravity as the Spanish
Junta or the Grand Council
of Venice."

--The Jesuit Lafitau

In a small restaurant north of the border, I was guzzling
coffee (Anguish), an omelet (Good Sense) and homemade
bread (Fulfillment)—oh and butter (Panache) wrapped
in pretty little silver squares, when I finally encountered J
again. He is called Jacques here. He was at the register
in a white shirt, a cigarette as usual fuming by his side. He
spoke the strange Canadian French to a passing customer,
then turned to greet me with a smile. I was just finishing
my repast, and nearly choked.
        "I thought you'd be here tomorrow," he said.
Where am I?
        "Near home. Lucky you had good weather.
        You made good time."
About fifty miles a day.
        "So that's good. Rain is due."
Rain.
        "Rain. I'll drive you."
He vanished through swinging doors into the kitchen, but I
only experienced a moment's panic.
Sadly, I was getting wise.
        "I can leave in an hour,"
        he said on his return.

A soft rain was descending outside now. Cars swished by.
The sweet bread & hot coffee were more healing to me
than the high air of a mountain chalet, or than the voice of
an old friend. This was the saddest part. Tears began
to join the rain in falling. The cook was curious.
I heard Jacques say:
        "She's all right. She's just remembering the
        assassination of President Kennedy."
He played American music on the car radio. I fell asleep,
but it was a mistake. Sleep is often a mistake. I jolted
awake in a state of perfect terror: comprehension. The sight
of his profile close by only made it worse.

You betrayed me, I said.
    "No, I didn't. Never."
You were the man sent to lead me from the chalet.
You are part of the whole plot. You!
    "It's not a plot, it's a test."
You son of a bitch.
    "Listen, Oneida, listen," he said, "Remember
    the couple escaping from East Berlin into
    the Western sector, in the dead of the night,
    in the forest, not long ago? The father
    was carrying the child and the child began
    to cry. And the father put his hand on the
    child's mouth to quiet him, and when
    he got, safely, to the other side, he
    discovered he had suffocated his child?
    Remember?"
No.
    "Yes, you do. Well, you represent to me that
    man and his child. On the one hand you
    want to escape your history and all social
    responsibility, and at the same time you are
    destroying your child's chance at growth."
Don't listen! cried the Virgin Mary: Anyone who speaks
of 'growth' is a phoney and should be blown away.
Don't listen.
I blocked my ears at once and began to concentrate on
some questions I had been harboring for some time:

(1)   When Shakespeare referred to sleep as "great Nature's
second course," did he mean "dessert" or "second route"?

(2)   When Shelley wondered, "Can spring be far behind?",
didn't he really mean "ahead"?

(3)   In that song that goes, "Oh don't deceive me, Oh never
leave me, how could you treat a poor maiden so?"—Is

the maiden describing herself as "poor" because she has little money, or because she is unloved?

(4)   If Jesus was drunk (but who said he *was*) when he tipped over those tables, does it mean a person should be a little tipsy in order to act with courage and honesty?

But then I knew we had crossed the border and were back in the United States of America again. I felt in my gut a gravity I associate with this continent. Bones under the flesh of earth, bumpy mountains, a river on the right, the excess of everygreen. If you see the smoke, you can't see the fire, she said. I took my fingers out of my ears.

Where are we?
          "Near Jackman," said Jacques, "and that's
          the Kennebunk River, as you must know."
As I?
          "Must know."
He pulled the car to the side of the road, a bobwhite whistled Bob White. Trees, smoke. We stared at each other.
          "I'll leave you off here."
Leave me?
          "Off."
Here?
          "Just walk down that slope there."
I opened the car door, and he didn't try to stop me. He was being polite. "Goodbye," I said, "Lopez," and my eyes blurred. But I didn't let him see. Slammed the car door, and stood stock still, staring, in my mind's eye at the words, "Goodbye, Phoney." They had a certain ring.

GOODBYE

great jubilation that follows a stern goodbye must spring
from righteousness or the plasticity of the balloon surro
e Globe. What else can explain the fervor of soldiers or
solution of lovers to be faithful to each other though a
llion goodbyes are implied? So many words for "goodbye"
positive ring—"GOODbye"—"FareWELL"—"ADIOS"—"SEE you"
unctive with the straight posture of righteousness. Just
eing done. The enemy is anyone, who happens to require t
But how can you say goodbye to part of your character? A
he person who has influenced you the most is the one leas
with. A traitor to your cause! The Underminer. Enters
eams with a laturn, again & again, immortal. And when y
bye to this person, yea, you feel brilliant. No one can
ou around. It's the end. There's the void, hurray, no m
ormer of your Destiny. No more bully! Free at last, one
ee, four. But if you can't help looking back, just once,
f he is suffering, you discover, nay, he's cold as ice, c
less. He's got something else on his mind. Your victory
litude, c'est tout.

And so it was, goodbye, for good, as I crossed down the slope,
stinging. I had scoured the wool of the Lamb till the blood
sprang up from its skin! I looked around wildly for the
Virgin but she had fled, babbling.

Below me lay meadows familiar and green. As summer is
announced by buttercups and daisies, so the downward
curve is heralded by memorabilia—the faces of old friends,

photographs, a letter, a bit of jewelry. I knew I was close
to home, but I was frightened at the slight increase in
speed that entered my timing—
fifteen minutes were more like ten.

But I plunged forward across the pasture towards the
river, and there discovered my parents' trailer, a rusty
shell, like the skeleton of a big prehistoric insect.
I didn't like it. Bees had built their nests there. The kitchen
table was rotten and cocoons bubbled between its legs.

I pried around, looking for some old familiar object—a shoe,
a plate, a bottle of Muscatel—but only found some
squashed-up magazines, Kennedy's face like a pile of grey
mashed potato under the convertible couch.

Then it was that I heard a plaintive male wail in the
distance, like the sound one is said to hear arising from
poronographic encounters on Forty Second Street,
like a siren. It went through one ear and out the other, as I
stood there, like a shell. My soul left my body.

I was staring at a dog.
A very old wretched hound, yellow.
It was staring at me.
It did not growl, but stood immobile, as did I.
Spittle lathered its black lips.
Its eyes were glazed, as were mine.
Then I went down on my knees and held out my arms.
Yellow, I said. Yellow wagged his tail, or switched it,
cautiously.
Come here, boy.
The obedient beast, my old dog, came over and sank down

on his belly, drooling and panting.
I rubbed and fondled him, and my soul returned to my
body.

Slowly, in the background, that plaintive wail returned,
and the dog and I set off towards the river, leaving
behind the wrecked trailer. I felt, with the dog at my side,
safe, and close to happiness. I knew I would not be lacking
human company much longer, and paused in the long
green grass, to enjoy this strange sensation. From where we
stood I could see the river. Brown and packed with
timber—logs spread out all the way across the water, solid
as Abraham Lincoln's cabin wall. A thin blue line of
smoke was rising off to the left, in a cluster of trees,
and we moved on.

Existential moment!
Holy Moly!
Shazam!

Existential moment!
Holy Moly!
Shazam!

There was a little group of people beside a campfire.
Someone was playing a radio. Hard rock. A yellow
helicopter was sitting on the grass on the opposite bank of
the river. My dog and I parted the veils of smoke,
and at first I saw the three awful men—Mister Poole, the
Right Reverend Canon Brooke and Doctor Water—
performing unmentionable acts upon each other.
I was shocked.

I shielded my eyes and looked across the river and saw,
beside the helicopter, my daughter and Sergeant Pepper,
holding fieldglasses, rifles strapped to their thighs,
looking my way. When Pepsi saw me seeing her, she jumped
up and down, frantically signalling. Whether it was a
welcome or a warning I couldn't tell, but I decided to
proceed as I had from the beginning—on my own, alone.
Taking directions from no one!

At that moment, the Canon saw me. He hastily pulled up
his pants and nudged the other two, but they were
preoccupied. They would not look up. Canon, then,
lunged towards me, fumbling with his fly.
    "What the hell do you think you're doing?"
Just looking around.
    "So buzz off."
No way, I'll do what I want.
    "You want to die?"
Some things are worse than death, I said.
    "Like what?"
Slavery, torture, losing someone you love—

"You are one pompous bitch."

Reverend!

"Let me tell you something," he hissed and
shoved me up against a tree. "Where you are
standing now used to be Acadian territory.
And on this very spot, a hundred people,
mainly women and children, were
tomahawked and tortured in their beds, by
your race. About thirty houses were
burned to the ground. But you know what?
The Church was spared. That's right.
The Church was spared."

Really?

"Really."

Well, why do you think people risk that kind of death, if
dying is the worst thing that can happen?

"Because death is the definition of life."

Is this how you justify sexual liberty?

"I don't have to justify anything. One must,
in this life, occasionally veer off,
experiment."

An hour doesn't last forever, but it can corrupt forever.

"The hour of your death lasts forever, and
you're about to discover this."

I'd like to make one more point.

"This is not a debating society!"

I glanced around the tree quickly and saw the other two
fellows in positions of maximum depression, which is
often called fulfillment. Then I raised my eyes to the
boughs of the tree, where I felt Her presence protecting
me. Sure enough, she was up there, lounging on a branch
with an apple. The Reverend squeezed my arm.

"I bet I know what would be worse than
death for you," he said.

Uh uh. I know what your're thinking, and you better forget it.

"You're celibate, am I correct?"

Correct.

"That's abnormal."

I know.
My dog was beginning to get kind of surly, given the
Reverend's actions against my body. He showed his fangs
all covered in spit and growled. This alarmed the man,
he slackened his grip, and for a second I felt sorry for him.
Such a weak heap of flesh and appetite!
Did you kill Selwyn? I asked him.

> "Your old man did that. He is helping us
> eliminate certain elements from society. He
> does it for his reasons, we do it for ours,
> but we can cooperate."

But surely you disagree with his goals!

> "Goals are irrelevent. You must know that.
> Goals are vapors. Facts are facts."

Why are you killing people?

> "It improves the landscape." He smiled
> softly. "I am an ecologist. I would shoot an
> Eskimo before I let an Eskimo shoot a
> little white baby seal. So cute!"

And what about my old man? Why does he do it?

> "That's what we wanted his papers for, silly.
> To find out. Now come on. Please?"

Motherfucker.

> "Right on!" cried the Virgin from on high.

I did Shoot-Tiger-and-Brush-Knee-and-Push in two swift
moves, knocking the Reverend over. Then I ran to the
river, as fast as I could, the dog at my heels, we leaped from
log to log, slipping, getting wet, but not without some
grace. I thought of Eliza crossing the ice! I thought of certain
historical victories. I could hear Pepsi cheering me on,
but for her I only felt Rage.

Hello, baby bitch, I said in greeting—
then whopped her on the butt til my hand was aching and
she was crying. She rushed to Sgt. Pepper for sympathy
but was knocked away, as the woman was picking off

the three men on the other side of the river with her rifle
full of buckshot. Pepsi ran from the East to the West,
wailing, then leaped into the helicopter.

If you think you're free, you're crazy, I screeched.

She was reduced further, and I climbed in the helicopter
beside her, feeling a dash of pity for her seasonal confu-
sion, then whopped her again, so that the familiar might
become mundane. We stared at each other in silence.
Then Sgt. Pepper joined us in the helicopter, as did Yellow
the dog. And we took off, rising, roaring over the river
and the trees. The puff of smoke below gave way to thin
mountain air. I craned my neck to get one last look at
that haunted terrain. On the right (West) a deep river,
black and thick. On the left (East) green sloping fields.
We curved East along the coastline then.

I saw the Virgin approaching a cloud bank, one hand
extended—pointing down, Southeast, to the sea's edge.
Her other sign was raised in the V sign for Victory.

And there below I saw a stony jetty. Like a chameleon, dark
and green from the sea's slime, curling around. It was the
size of a crack in a prison wall and the size of the whole
continent. The shape of a question mark. But nothing was
obvious. I couldn't exactly call it mine. Only my
gravestone would be really mine, the only rock to build my
house upon. And so, from her winning smile, the Virgin
implied as much, the same, shrugging for a fall.

"Do you have any questions?" asked my pilot.
Only one, the usual one. Why? Why.

"I don't know why we do these things," she
had to admit, "We render unto Castro the
things that are Castro's, but then there's
always something left, something utterly
perverse. It rises up from nowhere, the
need to play games."

I don't like it.

"Sorry," she concluded.

So then I turned to my daughter and told her the price she
would have to pay for participating in the world's
corrupt activity. She would have to be tutored all summer.

"Oh Mom!" she wailed, but I raised my hand
in protest.

"Now listen," said Sgt. Pepper, "your friend
Mary said one thing the same as her son.
That is: *Have salt in yourselves and peace
with one another.*"

I looked at the face in the window, and the hand of the
Virgin, giving us the finger.

The Virgin shouted: "I said no such thing!"
I said, *Have salt on your shelf for your margarita.*

From on high the landscape looked nearly deserted, which
it was, so far north. As we travelled southwards, though,
small villages sprang up, highways, crowded harbors.
We were coming home.

And so we did, descending by air in spirals, into the dank
center of human vapors. Since then, my daughter has gone
to live on a hypothetical continent with others of like
mind. Later she may join me again on mine. Who can say?

New old leaves blow around my car, twirling in spirals
through the artificial sites and parks of this particular
island. The views are always the same, but appear to lie at a
greater distance than when I first came here.

Pressure, we all agree, is often put on the laboring force
in the island, and energy is released, sometimes violent,
sometimes benign, until that pressure is removed again,
by the rich and powerful perhaps. Daily we anonymous
many lose more and more, including our children, our jobs,
our lovers, our health and trust, until we are left only
with our understanding of Thermodynamics
(order and disorder).

Spiraling inwards, I know the end is near, a void more
natural than nature itself. And between said nature is
gravity, invisible, anonymous, and justice.

FICTION COLLECTIVE
Books in Print:

Fiction Collective books, catalogues, and subscription information may be obtained directly by mail from: Coda Press, Inc., 700 West Badger Road, Suite 101, Madison, WI 53713. Bookstores: Order through George Braziller, Inc., One Park Avenue, New York, NY 10016.